Their dream vacation will change their lives forever.

RA ANDERSON

BOOKS BY RA ANDERSON

CHILDREN'S

Once Upon the Rhine
(Cody the Cockatrice Series Book One)

The Land of Vikings & Trolls
(Cody the Cockatrice Series Book Two)

Puffins Take Flight
(Iceland: The Puffin Explorers Book 1)

Puffins Off the Beaten Path
(Iceland: The Puffin Explorers Book 2)

Puffins Encounter Fire & Ice
(Iceland: The Puffin Explorers Series Book 3)

Iceland: The Puffin Explorers Book of Fun Facts

ICELAND: The Puffin Explor-
ers Series Complete Set

YOUNG ADULT

Lakehouse Déjà Vu

The Last Crabtree Girl

Girl Sailing Aboard the Western Star

ALL READERS/COFFEE TABLE

If Pets Could Talk: A Service Dog

If Pets Could Talk: Farm Animals

If Pets Could Talk: Cats

If Pets Could Talk: Dogs

Thank you, Jessica Rose, for the use of your names
and your beautiful essence that allowed me to create
two beautiful characters and bring them to life.

To my family for always believing in me.

To Jukebox the Ghost: Tommy, Ben,
and Jesse, thanks for letting the girls
have fun singing "Cheers!"

PROLOGUE

ROSE AND JESSICA WERE DRAWN to each other from the first moment they met nine years ago while in middle school, not because of any specific similarities but by curiosity and their differences. Rose's family had moved into town from the Caribbean, fresh off a sailboat, and her only friend was her cat who came with them from the boat. She looked like a surfer girl coming in after a full day riding the waves, with her untamed, curly, sun-bleached hair, sparkling green eyes that could be seen across a room, and her frame so tiny she looked to be a grade or two below Jessica.

Jessica was beautiful inside and out. She was outgoing and adventurous and loved traveling to Europe with her parents on vacations and all the ventures that came with those trips, like shopping in Paris. Her family lived in a huge Kentucky antebellum house built in the 1830s and remodeled right before Rose moved to town. The old plantation land had been used as a corn, hay, and dairy farm for most of the 1900s. It was sold to a developer who subdivided it in the late 1990s and then surrounded the antebellum house with dozens of homes built on large five- to ten-acre lots in the 2000s. Jessica's family home was the largest lot in the subdivision, allowing a six-stall horse barn and two nice size pastures nestled in the backyard with large oak trees and a small lake. Her family had hired help to care for the horses, land, and barn. The grass rolled with the small hills, lined with a black wood fence that separated their land from the other lots.

Together in high school, these stunning young ladies didn't notice the boys trying to get their attention because they only had eyes for their four-legged "true loves" grazing in the fields.

While Jessica had to focus on riding and training with her horse instructor, preparing for her next horse show, Rose was always present with a journal in her hand, only putting it down to groom and ride with Jessica when she wasn't training.

Journaling had become a habit for Rose early in life. She enjoyed logging significant and not-so-important information, personal thoughts, and strategies to achieve goals as well as records of her accomplishments, but most importantly, it helped her lay her emotions out on paper and stop her from feeling overwhelmed. Growing up on a sailboat, she'd lived like more of a minimalist, not needing things to place on shelves to remember adventures of any kind. Her fondest memories of her youth, before Jessica, were sailing, star gazing, and scuba diving. Her parents had decent jobs and no one felt like they were missing out, yet her parents didn't buy Rose a car nor could they afford the luxury of a horse. Rose rode Jessica's horses, and Jessica's parents gave Rose a horse to call her own, telling her she was a "natural rider." Though she couldn't handle the pressure of being in the "spotlight" that would have come with competing with Jessica, she definitely enjoyed the one-on-one bond between horse and rider and loved cheering for Jessica at her horse shows.

When it was time to turn the page and begin the next chapter in life, going off to college, they did so together and, without hesitation, chose to be roommates. That's what best friends do. Every inch of Rose was delighted that Jessica wanted to attend the University of Kentucky because it was less than a couple of hours away from home and they could drive home to ride every weekend if they wished. The thought of being close to family and Jessica's farm was comforting. And Jessica loved driving them home in the new car she'd gotten for her high school graduation gift from her grandparents. They also enjoyed cruising around town with the convertible top down, and any occasion in the car was a chance to sing in the wind again.

Jessica studied science, thinking of becoming a veterinarian. Her study groups were important to her, and she flitted in and out of their room and made time for parties, new friends, and her busy social life. Rose knew she wanted to one day run her own business, so was aiming for a dual degree in business and psychology and dedicated to her studies. She spent countless hours in classes, usually at the desk in their shared dorm room or at the library with her nose in textbooks, but mostly alone, and that's how she preferred life. Both overextended themselves, nearing the hours and classes needed to graduate early on about the same timeline, and thus had little time for their regular weekend trips back to the farm to ride and de-stress. They hadn't realized how hard this semester would be, how much they missed their weekends with the horses, and when it came time to prepare for finals, they talked about spring break and how they both desperately needed a respite. Surprisingly enough, they both decided not to go home, wanting to do something different and go somewhere they'd not been before.

Like a shining star, Jessica was the picture next to the word *outgoing*. There were no strangers in her path, while Rose preferred to stay in her "safe place" and it was hard for her to look anyone in the eye. But Jessica had a plan! She was taking Rose to Florida. They would have an amazing time and the break from routine they both needed while maybe also helping Rose open up and enjoy life more. It would be incredible—a trip that would change her life forever! That's the part that's unexplainable, though. Deep down, Jessica felt as if she knew both their lives would be changed, but not *how*. How could Jessica plan a trip that's so mind-blowing it would be life altering? Jessica could only hope that, however it worked out, it helped Rose bloom like the beautiful flower she was.

Unbeknownst to Rose, Jessica had accidentally seen an upsetting post in Rose's journal about her deepest fears and then gone to work devising her plan. While they did research the trip together, Jessica did some extra digging on her own and found the perfect spot with a little help from her parents' travel planner, their Fairy Trip Mother. A B&B located on a chain of lakes in central Florida was the perfect spot. A true getaway! Sun, water sports, pool with meals included, plus planned day adventures to the beach and to see Florida's wildlife. One day sitting in their dorm room, Jessica opened the website on her computer, took in a deep breath, and turned to Rose.

"Rose, what about this place? I was thinking outside the box," Jessica said to Rose as she turned her computer screen toward Rose. It read, *Lakehouse Déjà Vu B&B*.

The B&B was owned and operated by an older couple, Mr. and Mrs. Jones, and the website displayed a beautiful photograph of the couple standing out on a dock with a large house behind them that had lots of windows. The site also invited guests to use any of their "water toys," and pictured was a ski boat, a couple of people jet skiing, and a sailboat sailing across the large lake. It also advertised their connections with the Save the Manatee Club and gave a link to their website. The B&B owners could set up a private guided kayaking tour to see Florida's wildlife on the St. Johns River with the Save the Manatee Club, where guests could see several manatees gather near the warmth and stable temperatures of the natural spring at Blue Springs State Park.

"It looks awesome!" Rose replied as she began to read more.

This was Florida, off the beaten path, not the typical beach party or theme park spring break Rose thought Jessica would choose. Rose would read a book and take her journal, knowing there would be plenty to write about. Jessica would take a bathing suit for every occasion, planning for time on the water, lots of time in a lounger, soaking up the sun, and maybe a trip or two to the beach.

"This will be my first time as an adult on vacation," Rose said, a little unsure of what she was agreeing to.

"We can see the horses most weekends, but we can't go on a vacation or get away for a week any other time. I will start my internship as soon as the semester ends, and you will be working as well, and it's Florida—the sunshine state! What do you think?" Jessica hoped it was enough to convince Rose.

"I agree we should try adulting for spring break. I've been feeling a little guilty about Mom doing all my laundry at home, and last spring break was great, but I think I did more studying at home than anything," Rose admitted. "Wait! Why do you want to go to this B&B and not some party beach or Universal Studios?"

"I've been to the theme parks, and sitting on a beach for a full week is just too much. I want to hang out with you, and the lake life sounds like fun. Plus, you can take me out on their sailboat. I've never done that before!" Jessica responded, truly meaning every word.

"This is supposed to be our adulting trip, but I have to ask Mom and Dad for the money for gas, food, and"—she looked down at her hands—"can we share a room to keep the cost down?" A hint of color filled Rose's cheeks as she spoke.

"Of course!" Jessica replied.

Jessica thought again about what she had read in Rose's journal. It weighed heavy on her thoughts. Journaling was the one thing Jessica had never understood about Rose. It wasn't like she was writing about boys—she was too painfully shy to get to know any, much less date. She wanted Rose to take a break from journaling, especially since she, herself, was willing to take a break from her newfound pastime of parties and dating. Jessica could find parties to attend any time, and she wasn't ready for a steady boyfriend, but she realized Rose needed her. Jessica couldn't wait to spend some time away from college with her; however, knowing Rose the way she did, she would be too proud to accept any type of handout, so she booked them each a room and paid ahead for as much of the "extras" as she could without letting Rose know. She wanted to give her best friend the kind of vacation her own family indulged in frequently, and this way they both would enjoy it together without feeling guilty.

CHAPTER 1

ADULTING

Tuesday, 23rd of March

"**W**E HAVE FEVERS OF A hundred and three," Jessica and I sang out over the '70s and '80s top hits, letting the songs fill the space between us and taking our minds away from our task at hand. We had books piled around us as we crammed for yet another midterm.

"Hot blooded, we are burning with envy!" we both sang out.

Realizing we'd both sung the same random lines and changed the words to the original song the same way, we looked at one another and laughed.

We watched as more students carried bags toward their cars, heading off campus for spring break. Our moods shifted, making it impossible to concentrate on school. My heart raced, pounding inside my chest. The jealousy of those students leaving was unbearable. My face reddened as another car jam-packed with students cheered and drove away.

Jessica and I have two more days of midterms. How can I possibly study while watching students skip town? The sunshine state was beckoning me. As I turned to look at Jess, I could see it in her eyes too. I preferred to study in the library or our dorm room, but even there I couldn't concentrate, so Jessica and I decided to study together and struggle to focus together.

Our suitcases had been packed and safely tucked away in the trunk of Jessica's cherry-red BMW convertible for a couple of days, and we'd been day-dreaming of our adventure ever since.

I dropped my book down on the grass and cried out to Jess, "Is it normal to have such a high spring fever? I'm unable to function like a normal human. The only medicine that could possibly work would be sun and fun."

Oh, I need spring break, but maybe it would be better if we spent our days at the barn, not at a B&B with strangers in Florida!

Dear Journal,

Our first trip as adults with no parental supervision. Jess and I scooped up a room on the B&B app, in a beautiful house located on a chain of lakes in central Florida, and it has a picturesque pool like you would see at the homes of the rich and famous! The road trip will be a long one, but Jess wants to drive the whole way.

College is overwhelming sometimes. I should be reading my PSY202 notes on the scientific study of behavior and experience and motivation. I need some motivation to get on with it. Another hiccup in my study plans, my psychology professor snuck this into my brain and now it's there for the long haul. She said:

"If you feel as if you don't fit into this world, it's probably because you're here to create a better one."

Then she reminded us that we will begin studying empaths and HSP (highly sensitive person) after the break. Apparently, an empath sees the world differently than others and is highly aware of the emotions of those around them. Sometimes they feel the pain of others to the point of having acute fatigue and physical ailments. I am not sure why this study topic has choked out my ability to function, but the more she explained what an empath is, the more it hit home.

I am an empath!

How do I survive? How can I be compassionate without absorbing the stress of others and the world around me? I have no tools to help me. I am feeling overwhelmed. Is this why I need to hide from the world?

I should go for a walk—no, a jog. But I am too tired. Help! I need spring break, any break, now!

Feeling: Like a wilted Rose!

Tossing my book back into the dorm room, I left to take a much-needed stroll outside. As I walked along the courtyard, taking deep breaths and ridding my mind of chaos, I knew I needed to call home. I'd tried calling home only a couple of times a week, so my parents didn't worry about me missing them too much. It was the opposite for most college students. They called home only when they needed more money or if they were in trouble. Jessica called her parents at least once a week to check in, plus we both enjoyed driving home at least once a month to ride. Me, well, I didn't like change, and the comfort of hearing my parents' voices calmed me, so I struggled with staying away. When Jessica talked me into the Florida trip, I told her I thought it was a great idea and couldn't wait to go. Inside, though, I was trying to put on my big girl panties and suck it up to go have fun beyond my comfort zone. She wanted me to go so bad, and maybe it would be "life changing," but my gut screamed *stay home*. I kept that to myself, not even writing it in my journal.

A buzz came from my pocket, sending a tickle down my leg. I reached for my outdated iPhone and smiled at my mother's face. It was almost as if she knew what I was thinking. *Oh no, let's hope not.*

"Hi, Mom!"

"Rose! Have you made a packing list and double checked it? Do you have enough money? I can put more in your account if you need it. And remember the weather changes every hour there…"

"Yes, Mom, I have enough money. I have my emergency credit card, and I will remember my phone. But, Mom—"

"…and please don't forget your phone and call me every day," Mom worried on as if she hadn't heard me at all.

"I will let you know when we get there, but I am an adult now and don't need to check in with you every day or every moment of every day. We will be fine!" It did feel odd trying to convince my mother to let me do adult things while feeling like a child when needing to ask for money. Adulting in college was quite a challenge!

"But, dear, I am not done," Mom said to Dad as her voice grew distant.

Dad's voice confirmed he had taken the phone from her as he said firmly, "Rose, I want you to take extra cash with you just in case and you do need to call us every night before you go to bed."

"Dad, did you trust me when I was eight to take a night shift sailing our boat in the middle of nowhere?"

"Well, yes, but—"

"Well then, please trust Jess and me to drive down to central Florida for a week's vacation as adults."

"Well, don't forget to trade off driving. That's a

long drive for you two," Dad continued, sounding a little defeated.

"Yes, we will take turns, and it's a new car, so you don't have to worry about it breaking down on the side of the road."

"Print off your triple-A card. If you break down or have a flat tire, pull way off to the side and call their number. People drive way too fast on the highways, and you don't need to be on the side of the road…"

Oh, how I shouldn't have said anything about being on the side of the road, broken down.

"Pull off to the right of the highway and move far enough on the shoulder that you can open the driver's door and not have it swing out near the cars driving—"

I blurted out, "Yes, Dad."

"You know what, don't even get out on the driver's side. Crawl out the other side," Dad continued.

"Yes, Dad," I said again.

"Then walk farther away from the road and then call triple-A," Dad added.

"Yes, Dad," I said yet again.

"And call me—maybe *before* you call triple-A."

He continued, but I had to blurt out, "Okay! Dad! We will be fine!" I hoped I didn't sound disrespectful, but at the same time, I had to let him know I'd heard him the first dozen times.

After we ended the phone call with several "I

love you toos," I wondered if all young adults went through the same thing, if their calls home were the same. But the truth was, my parents were right. I was nervous about going on a vacation without them too. Jessica was my very best friend, but she was also the type of person you couldn't argue with. What would I do if she wanted to go to bars, parties, or hook up with boys while we were in Florida? That just wasn't me. How long would it take for her to become bored of the B&B's lake life and enjoying nature? How could I be worried and excited at the same time?!

Quickly my hand found my gold ship chain necklace around my neck, and I ran my fingers over its smooth surface a few times, waiting for my heart to slow to its normal rhythm. I wrapped my arms around my stomach, clenching against the butterflies stirring up there as I began the short walk back toward the dorm.

When I arrived back in our room, Jess was already there, applying a little makeup and glancing down at some study notes while waiting for her date. I couldn't imagine going on a date with these thoughts swirling in my mind. Well, truth be told, I couldn't imagine going on a date at all without feeling the world roll and my stomach surge. I felt my face warm at thinking about speaking with a boy. I simply wouldn't know what to say.

Slipping into my desk chair, I opened my journal and wrote:

I must release fear, lead my life based on love and trust. My impression of me being an empath is greater in this second because I *feel* my parents' fears and hesitation for letting me grow up. I have enough fear all on my own—including speaking to young men. There is no need to load more on me.

CHAPTER 2

CHEERS

Friday Morning, 26th of March

"CAR KEYS, HAT, WALLET WITH credit card, bathing suits, sandals—check. That's all I need. Looks like I am ready for this vacation!" Jessica said as she folded her long, slender legs and almost six-foot frame into the driver's seat. She slid her finger over a button, and the soft black convertible top slowly folded down, exposing us to the early morning sunlight and the chill of the Kentucky spring air. "Rose, I'll drive. You look exhausted," she added, projecting feelings onto her co-pilot.

But it was true—I was spent.

Jessica buckled in, stared at her reflection in the rearview mirror, and grinned as she slid her dark tinted sunglasses up her nose to hide her sapphire blue eyes. She shifted the car into drive, stepped on the gas, raised both hands in the air, and yelled, "Wooo hooo!"

We laughed in unison as we felt the power of her new car push our bodies deeper into the seats. Her long blonde hair fluttered behind her as if she were in a movie. Unlike my long, brown, messy, curly hair that smacked my face as the wind swirled it into dreadlock-like rolls. Then, as if my hair were octopus tentacles, it tried to position itself as if hanging on by looping around my head. It had somehow come to life and was trying desperately to jump from the car or hang on for dear life, but not sure which it preferred. At first I used both hands to try controlling the knotted rolls of hair and flailing curls from flapping into my eyes and invading my mouth and swept escaping strands away from getting stuck in the creases of my lips. At the last stop light before merging onto the highway, I finally managed to wrangle the mess up into a high ponytail. When I felt Jessica's gaze on me, I turned toward her as she glanced back at the road and then back toward me. Our eyes met, and we laughed until we almost cried.

We waved our goodbyes to no one like the other students had done when leaving the campus, then we focused on enjoying the distance grow between us and the university. Jessica slid her finger over the volume button, and the music danced around us with the wind.

I reached down between my feet and heaved my

large carry bag onto my lap where it filled the entire space between me and the dash. Digging around, I found my sunscreen, flipped the visor down in search of a mirror, and applied the SPF 70 all over my lightly freckled face until the lotion disappeared. When I replaced the lid, I decided to organize and check my bag to make sure I hadn't forgotten anything. Journal, face sunscreen, all-over sunscreen, Chapstick with sunblock, extra floppy hat, snacks, mints, pens, phone and charger, regular hand lotion, hand sanitizer, my sun protection hoodie, and scarf, tissues, sunglasses—

Feeling Jess's eyes on me, I looked up and saw her smiling and laughing while glancing down at my bag. She had a phone with a wallet magnet on the case, and I had a bag large enough for my five-foot, ninety-eight-pound body. I could practically sleep inside of it.

"I think I left the B&B's information in the printer tray," I said and then repeated twice for her to hear me over the upgraded sound system and the wind.

Finally, as the song faded, she acknowledged me. "No worries. It's on the app!" she yelled back with a giggle.

It's a fact that I like printing important information out just in case something happens to our phones, and she was always confident that they would be with us and working.

Softly we heard, "Here's to more of the *everyday*," catching both of our attention.

"Oh, Jukebox the Ghost!" Jessica shrieked. She cranked up the volume and held one arm up in the air as if holding a champagne glass while trekking south on I-75.

We started singing along with our favorite band, our voices carrying into the wind in unison as we sped down the highway.

> "Raise a glass and sing along
> The outcasts and the underdogs
> On the benches, on the sidelines
> Wallflowers, this is our time
> Ordinary people every day
> In the nosebleeds, in the bleachers
> I see victors, I see fighters..."

We looked at one another and smiled, raising our pretend glasses high above our heads, and continued belting out lyrics along with Tommy, Ben, and Jesse's band.

> "Raise a glass and cheers to every day
> Raise a glass to more of the everyday
> Cheers
> Cheers
> Cheers to all the dreamers, the everyday believers
> Cheers
> Cheers
> Cheers to all the dreamers..."

We kept on singing into the wind as we cruised

south down the highway, leaving behind our everyday troubles and this past week's midterms. After several long hours had passed, along with Tennessee and Georgia, which included several towns, rivers, farms, and cities, I pointed at the *Welcome to Florida* sign. We both smiled and yelled, "Florida, here we are!" Then I signaled for Jess to pull into the rest stop so we could stretch and switch places. As we slowed and looked for a parking spot, the convertible top began to close around us.

Stepping out of the car, we heard children screaming with excitement. They ran from one picnic bench to another, chasing each other. All were dressed in bright neon matching shirts with big black hand-painted ears painted across the front. I thought about what a magical vacation they must have been on, and how I'd felt the same way when we first got in the car. We walked for a few minutes, stretching our bodies, and used the facilities before returning to the car. I jogged around the car twice, trying to stay ahead of road fatigue.

"It's okay, Rose. I want to keep driving, at least for another hour or so," Jess said in her familiar tone that conveyed she was not going to budge on this decision. "I'm too pumped up to rest, and I am having fun driving."

"Okay! When you get bored, I will be glad to take over," I replied.

She returned a smile, started the car and pushed

the button to put the convertible top down as we pulled out of the parking spot, then sped back onto the highway and cranked up the stereo. "Heading down the highway! Listen to us go, yea!" she yelled into the wind, making some lyric changes to the classic rock song by Steppenwolf.

I pulled drinks from the cooler, and we raised our cream soda bottles. "May you always be my compass, the one who guides me to eternal bliss," Jess said, and then I added, "And to lots of Florida fun. Cheers!" and we clanked our bottles together.

After first seeing our parents making a toast together when we were young, we hadn't missed an opportunity to make our own toasts with any drink we opened. Our toasts had evolved through the years. I think our first one was something like, "Cheers to us dreamers, and to us, the young believers." Maybe this was the reason behind Jukebox the Ghost's song "Cheers" meaning so much to us?!

The songs soon faded and mixed with the sounds of cars and trucks rolling down the highway alongside us. Soon all the sounds were washed away by the thoughts haunting my mind. I sat and dug inside my bag for my phone and realized I hadn't downloaded the books I'd wanted to read. Apparently when I was packing, reading had been the last thing I wanted to do, but I desperately needed something now to tune the thoughts of meeting people at the B&B and what if we didn't like it, what happens then. My necklace was cool and soft between my fingertips, the little links draped down over my fingers, and as I moved, they would snap up, taking turns between my thumb and index finger. My fingers moved back and forth as I thought more about the B&B and the people we would have to meet. I remembered the photo of their library and how the bookcase reached the ceiling of the second floor. Books galore! I could read while sitting out by their pool, but that wasn't helping me now. I kicked my bag back down around my feet and set my phone on my lap after playing today's Wordle game and thought of texting Mom and Dad but didn't.

The B&B was only a few miles from the Clermont exit off the turnpike, and Jess had programmed the address into her phone while we were at the rest area, so I didn't need to worry over helping her navigate. Instead, I thought about all we knew about where we were going and all that I didn't yet know. We didn't plan our days out, and I wasn't sure what to do without a schedule. I glanced over at Jess, looking as if she was ready to hit Florida like an off-season hurricane.

Watch out, Florida, here comes Hurricane Jessica! Hold on, Rose, don't let your petals fly off.

With the wind in our hair and music in our ears, we drove on for another hour or so until my eyes felt heavy. Jess glanced over and grinned at me when I reclined my seat and then rested my head against the door, tucked away from the flapping wind.

I will be rested up when, or if, she wants me to drive.

Soft buzzing and pulsing, slow beeping sounds gradually woke me. Lifting my arm off my lap, I reached over to tap Jessica to turn the car alarm off, but the seat was vacant. I wiped off the drool so unpleasantly running down the side of my chin. The BMW was parked, no more wind, no loud music, and no Jess. I could faintly hear water dripping, splashing, and bubbling, and then it was gone. The soft humming, throbbing, pumping tones grew louder, and I could feel pain all over my body. Holding onto the car door as if I were holding on for dear life, every muscle ached from sleeping for hours in this strange position. How could I have slept that hard in a convertible, with the wind swirling and flapping around us and the music turned up so loud?

My vision blurred as if I was sitting in a thick haze.

It must be Florida's afternoon showers.

I'd heard you could almost set your watch to them, so maybe it had rained, causing the fog to settle around me. The steam from the ground ascended, and I was having difficulties focusing my gaze. I'd thought we would arrive at the B&B in the early evening. I squinted, and my eyes burned. White rays seemed to shine down from high noon, maybe one o'clock, but with the clouds, I couldn't tell the time. It could easily be the sun setting. I patted my pockets again for my phone.

Where did I put my phone?

One could only assume Jessica hadn't been able to wake me when we'd arrived. I must have been sound asleep, but why would she leave me in the car, alone? Because I was out cold, I guessed. Midterms had been more difficult than I'd realized. My mind hadn't settled yet from all my acquaintances, or fellow classmates and dorm occupants, using me like their doormat to get things off their chest. I'd been a sponge, soaking up their anxiety as they were letting it go. I'd found myself completely overwhelmed, which could explain why I was so exhausted. Being spent would explain why I'd slept through a windstorm at a rock concert, also known as Jess's convertible.

My gaze settled on the lake house as my brain fog began to lift and the water sprinklers dripped from their timer turning them off. Nestled in front of the tall front windows was a tall bronze water fountain dripping and splashing water down from tier to tier. The house looked exactly like the pictures on the website—a two-story yellow house, and I could see the pool and lake right through the large French doors.

Maybe Jess couldn't wait for me because she had

to use their facilities. I would have left me in the car too, in that case.

My body felt heavy and ached, so I stretched, which triggered a yawn. My fingers found the door latch, and I pushed it open. Letting my feet drop out of the car's frame, I lowered them slowly to the ground and stood. My legs shook, so I slowly steadied myself. Facing the house, my gaze followed the brick walk up to the front door, but my feet didn't move. I hoped Jess would pop outside soon, greet me, laugh at how hard I'd slept, and then grab my hand and show me around, or at least lead me to a bed. But no luck. Jessica didn't come outside. A ping of concern jolted through my body like an electric current, quickly allowing me to find the strength to go inside.

I'm truly hardwired to be nervous about everything.

As I headed toward the house, my worrisome brain began to imagine horrible scenarios. Jessica triggering the house alarm—this one alone set my mind racing. I had a quick vision of police carrying us away, under arrest for trespassing. I shook my head and giggled at my crazy thoughts, but I kept my focus on the house.

Be brave, Rose! But why do my feet feel like they are in sludge? Feet, move so we can go find Jess!

Well, if it had been her setting off an alarm, I guessed the police would have rolled into the driveway by then. But Jessica had the reservations on her phone, so I knew we would be fine. I started walking up the path to the front door, and the alarms faded to nothing. It must have been coming from a different direction, so my mind stopped racing. I could call Jess, and she could come get me at the door. With that thought, I shoved my hand in my pocket but remembered my phone wasn't there. I couldn't recall where or when I'd had it last, but it probably was between the seat and the center console. At that point, I just wanted to go into the house and find Jessica. The door to the house was slightly ajar, so I knocked and slid inside.

CHAPTER 3

MORNING SUNSHINE

Saturday, 27th of March

SWEAT DRIPPED FROM EVERY PART of my body, but I shook as if I were cold. My body seemed to need me to gasp for air, and when I breathed in, I didn't recognize any of the smells around me. Too afraid to open my eyes, I felt the bed underneath me.

I'm in bed?!

I slowly opened my eyes and tried desperately to remember yesterday. I'd been in Jessica's car. I'd slept. I'd walked into the B&B and heard Jessica's voice and someone else's greeting me, but nothing else seemed clear.

As my eyes focused on the room around me, nothing seemed familiar, but I knew Jessica had brought me there. As I turned over to my side and wrapped my arms around the softest pillow I had ever felt, I smelled the light, sweet fragrance of coffee. If my nose was right, it was the scent of my favorite flavored coffee that lingered in the air. I could hear Jessica giggle. She wasn't in the room with me, but I knew she was near.

Jess brought my favorite coffee?!

My body relaxed at realizing Jessica was close, but I hoped my memories of entering the house would come back before I made a fool of myself to the owners of the B&B. The room was softly lit by the morning sun peeking through the shades. It must have been a bright sunshiny day, because the sun felt intense coming through the small crack in the shade. As I looked around the room, a nautical scene gulfed up around me like the ocean itself. A sketch painting of a sailboat being carried through the swells with a huge spinnaker sail aloft. The boat danced across the waves and was lifted in the air by the sail and thrust of the wave. A Wyland whale tail print and bronze whale tail sculpture sitting on a shelf, one of my favorite prints of all time, reminded me of my deep connection to the ocean. I had forgotten until now.

Two of my most favorite artists! Their work is in this room.

Slowly I tossed back the sheets, sat up on the edge of the bed, and tried desperately to recall anything from the previous night. All I could remember was the fog. Or was I in a fog? I was so tired! I stood and walked across the bedroom, waiting for my memories to seep back into form. I could hear

Jessica's voice and laughter, and I let out my breath in relief, knowing she was near. But I dreaded the embarrassment of my not remembering anything from last night and hesitated going downstairs at all.

The layout of the room was like a suite, with a bedroom in one area and only a threshold splitting the room. I found two sitting chairs keeping a driftwood coffee table in place that was adorned with a painting of a sailfish bursting up from the ocean, either making a kill or throwing a hook from its mouth. Above it on the wall was an old, used nautical chart that had been beautifully framed. The bathroom door had a beautiful stained-glass sailboat in its center, and the doorknob was a bronze octopus. The tentacles reaching out made me think about my hair.

I can only imagine what my hair looks like this morning!

I noticed my bag sitting on the chair and my suitcase on the luggage rack near the bathroom door. While brushing my teeth, I heard unfamiliar voices and someone's alarm clock beeping and buzzing, and then I heard Jessica's voice again but couldn't make out what was being said.

I continued to admire the art on the shelves and the paintings that hung on the wall, pausing at two wonderful charcoal prints of manatees. These mammals were the cutest sea cows that grazed on seagrasses in brackish rivers and ocean waters, but

I'd recently read that this year alone, hundreds were dying here in Florida.

It would be cool if we can see real manatees while we are here, I thought as I made my way to the shower.

The bathroom was also nautical, boating lines with various ship knots tied and hung on the towel racks. The bath sheets and towel sets were navy blue with white stripes, and all the bath accessories were made with seashells or ship lines with knots. I felt guilty drying off and not keeping the bathroom in such ship-shape order.

Walking back into the bedroom, I found more sailboat and nautical items. They were everywhere in the room. I fingered my ship chain around my neck and let out a deep breath. The decor made me feel right at home, back on the sailboat with my mom, dad, and my cat, Bear. It hadn't been anything fancy, but it was home and I loved it. Moving away from the water, off the sailboat, had been a difficult adjustment, but after the school year had started, I'd found Jessica, and our friendship had been my biggest treasure. Jessica's family was the reason I had a horse and learned how to ride. I would have given up my love for all things nautical for our friendship and horses, but this room was like it came out of one of my dreams.

I could look at this stuff all day, but I should go join Jess!

Following the voices, I paused and looked toward the buzzing and pulsing sounds, then left it for someone else to worry about as I made my way down the stairs. In the kitchen I found a table with an individual-cup coffee maker. Several brands and coffee flavors were neatly arranged next to a variety of sugars and creamers. My favorite coffee, my favorite creamer, I was in heaven. I glanced up and noticed the view from the kitchen was to die for. The whole south wall was lined with full-length glass windows and sliding doors, and beyond, the lake glistened like a sheet of tiny diamonds.

"Make yourself at home. Grab a cup of coffee if you would like and come outside with us," came the voice of an elderly man sitting outside on the patio with Jessica.

I smiled back at him and glanced at Jessica before selecting my coffee pod. I topped my coffee off with some Reddi-wip, making it look café bought, and found my way to the patio. I had to pause and take in the breathtaking scene of the flower and vegetable gardens, a pool built for the rich and famous, a seven-foot-tall classic antique cherub-angel tiered water fountain, and the private boat dock out on Lake Minnehaha. Only puffs of clouds scattered the sky, and as far as I could tell, the temperature was somewhere between perfect and marvelous.

"Good morning, sunshine!" Jessica said with a glowing smile.

"Good morning!" I said back to her, smiling sheepishly and turning a few shades of pink. *How can Jess drive over eleven hours, hardly sleep, and wake up looking this good? But that's Jess for you—pretty close to perfect!*

Jessica's voice broke my thoughts. "This is Mr. Jones. He lives here—it's his B&B. He has been teaching me about the different shaped clouds in the sky," she chirped as if she was perfectly fine that early every morning.

I knew better. She was not a morning person, but we were away from school. She seemed cheerful, like before a morning ride, plus her excitement about being in Florida and done with midterms would probably last until we got back anyway.

"Nice to meet you. I hope you slept well," Mr. Jones said as he greeted me with a warm smile.

"I slept hard, that's for sure!" I replied as I made my way into a comfortable chair next to Jessica, placing her in the middle closer to Mr. Jones. "I love the nautical room. It's really lovely."

Jessica seemed to bounce in her seat as she said, "I am in the room next to you. You must see it! It is the Theme Park Room with antique treasures from Disney, Universal, Cypress Gardens, Busch Gardens, and SeaWorld! B&B&D! Bed, breakfast, and dinner only for the special guests. Oh, and we can play any of the instruments in the music room, read any books from the library, and they have dinner every night around six, if we want. We just have to let Mr. Jones know in the morning."

I stared questioningly at Jessica. We were supposed to share a room, but I couldn't find the words.

Mr. Jones smiled and said, "My wife is a good cook and loving woman, but she has been quiet lately. This stage of her life is a little unsettling, so if you see her, please give her some space."

I casually glanced around, trying to catch a glimpse of Mrs. Jones, but she was nowhere to be seen. I thought of my grandmother and how she had gone through lots of changes with getting older. *That must be it.* Or maybe she was like me, needing alone time because it was the only thing that reduced sensory overload. That had been the first thing that made me wonder if I was an empath when my professor brought it up.

I couldn't help rolling my eyes at myself for that thought, then leaned over slightly to Jessica and whispered, "I don't remember coming inside the house yesterday…at all! How did I get to my room?"

"You came in so tired. Mr. Jones took your bags, and I showed you to your room. Oh, and your parents know you are here. I already texted them!" Jessica whispered back. She looked as if she was holding back a giggle when I shook my head in disbelief, then shrugged her shoulders and turned to Mr. Jones.

Mr. Jones slowly rocked in his chair and nodded as he continued, "I will be helping you this week with the kayaks, the fishing poles, or anything else you may need around the house. All Florida lakes have alligators, so if you swim in the lake, be very aware of your surroundings. I will be working in the gardens, and if you are interested, you can join me. I enjoy showing people how we are somewhat 'homesteaders' living off the land, or at least we reutilize and recycle well and use solar power. It does keep our shopping to a minimum because we eat what we grow, and as Jessica here has noticed, I love sharing information." Mr. Jones smiled. His gaze left ours as he slowly looked around, nodding proudly toward all the hard work he had accomplished, this giving us the chance to glance around and take notice of the sailboat pulled up on the beach and the potted plants that lined the walk. He stood slowly and added, "About your stay here, remember to come to me if you need anything for your rooms or have any questions." He smiled, nodded slowly as if making sure we heard him, then headed back into the house with his empty coffee cup.

I forgot to tell Mr. Jones his alarm clock or something seems to be ringing obnoxiously upstairs. I guess he will hear it soon enough.

"Isn't this place great?" Jessica's words fell around me, as I looked out toward the lake and noticed the sun dancing on the water.

The birds chirped, and two squirrels chased one another across the yard from one oak tree to the next as I sipped my coffee and wondered about this more relaxed and settled Jessica. The Jess I knew was a person who must always dine in restaurants, find other people her age and flow with the crowd, and would sleep in as long as possible.

"Rose, did you hear me?" Jessica asked again.

"Yes! This place is more than amazing. My room is decorated in nautical everything, my favorite. Plus, I am drinking Community Coffee's Sugar-Dusted Beignet flavored coffee, which I thought was discontinued months ago. And who uses French Vanilla So Delicious organic creamer and whipped cream in their coffee but me? And wait! Did he say no mosquitoes?" Hoping it didn't sound like I'd snapped, I added, "I am so thankful we found this place and it fit in my budget, and that we are here, together."

Jessica smiled, leaned back into her oversized chair, and gazed out toward the lake.

It had been many years since I'd lived around oversized, yet stealthy, flying, blood-sucking insects. Growing up on a sailboat, my tolerance for those pests hadn't grown. I'd only become more allergic. Leaving the mosquitoes was one of the only things I'd been happy about when my parents told me we were moving off the boat.

Jessica wiggled in the chair, gaining my attention, then said, "I can't wait to hear how they live basically off the grid." Seeming to energize again, she looked back at me. "I am going to get my swimsuit and go check out the lake and dock. Come with me!" she added while practically floating happily into the house.

I wonder if Jess realizes "living off the grid"

basically means they grow their own food. They garden. In the dirt.

Following Jessica, I returned our coffee cups to the kitchen, rinsed them both, and placed them in the dishwasher after confirming the reversible sign said, Dirty Dishes. When I turned around, I thought I heard someone at the dining table on the far side of the room, possibly a cup being set on the hard wood and a chair creaking. No one was there, but I could feel a swell of sorrow, pain so deep, so intense, that it made me want to cry. I took a deep breath and glanced around the room before going upstairs to get my swimsuit and then meet Jessica outside.

That was weird, but maybe it's Mrs. Jones in the office where I can't see her.

As I walked into my nautical room, I ran my fingers across the glaze that protected the sailfish image on the table. Reaching for my phone sitting on the edge of the table, I saw that it had no cell service and only one bar of life left, so I plugged it in.

My parents knew we were there, and Jessica had said she wanted to unplug. She was really the only other person I texted besides Mom and Dad, and they knew where I was, so there was no need for my phone. I slipped my swimsuit on and threw my clothes back on, grabbed my journal, and headed out to the pool area where Jessica and Mr. Jones sat visiting like old friends.

I wish I was brave enough to turn strangers into long-lost family members like Jess does!

Dear Journal,

First day of spring break and I already feel rejuvenated and totally relaxed. It's almost as if Florida has wrapped its arms around me and the sunshine has kissed my cheek. Jess and I explored this beautiful B&B home today, and Mr. Jones, the older gentleman in charge here, has made it seem as if we are visiting Jessica's granddad.

It seems I wasted a lot of energy worrying about giant blood-sucking mosquitoes and getting sunburned from being outside all day. I must have applied just the right amount of sunscreen to protect me from the sun, and the gardens here magically repel the plasma drinking insect-predators. Mr. Jones took us on a garden tour while explaining about each of the plants they grow, and I found it most interesting when he showed us several plants that repelled mosquitoes. We also saw several planters with oregano and basil, which I hope means fresh spaghetti sauce in our near future. Lemongrass growing in large pots lines the sidewalks in front of dwarf citrus trees. Thyme is planted in the cutest critter-shaped pots near the sitting areas. It seems they have the same taste in animals as I do. They have rosemary designed, or pruned, into topiary shapes like spirals, trees, cones, balls, and my favorite, hearts.

I didn't realize how much I enjoy rosemary's fragrance until today.

We learned there is another trick to repelling bugs too. There is no standing water anywhere around the house other than Lake Minnehaha. All bodies of water are in constant motion, which explains why there is a fountain in the pool and the hot tub water runs off the ledge, cascading down into the pool, and the fountains are constantly flowing, and the bases are stocked with goldfish and minnows, which eat mosquito larvae. What a brilliant way to landscape a Florida home.

Mr. Jones invited us to help cook dinner, and we were happy to help, especially since Mrs. Jones was not feeling up to it. We picked vegetables from the garden, and we, or Mr. Jones, caught some fish off the dock to share. The seasonings were a blend of fresh-grown spices and a lemon picked from one of their fruit trees. This was my first time cooking over a fire pit, and it seemed to make the food taste better than ever. It's not the vacation I thought it would be, but as I see it, it's better. Only one stranger, and he has taken to Jessica like family. This is a safe place… Right?

Feeling: Don't Worry, Be Happy! Rose is going to be all right.

CHAPTER 4

FLOATING ON AIR

Sunday, 28th of March

MR. JONES'S ALARM CLOCK WAS faintly hooting and clunking again. Today it sounded farther away, farther than just down the hall in their room. It didn't wake me, but I wondered if Mr. and Mrs. Jones were having some hearing issues as well.

I shouldn't be the one to bring up that subject, so it's best I forget about it.

The sun softly twinkled through the blinds, and I wondered what time it was. But it didn't really matter—I was on vacation! I rolled over and hugged my new favorite pillow in the world when I realized something.

I didn't dream again last night! Well, not that I can remember.

Typically, I dreamed enough for a dozen people. It was like my brain didn't stop all night long, and my dreams were so vivid as if I were awake. If I'd written them all down, I probably would have psychoanalyzed myself for having such intense and elaborate dreams. But here, I had never slept so peacefully. It was as if I was floating on air and all my worries had been left behind.

I should ask Mr. Jones what kind of mattress this is and where can I get a pillow like this one!

My gaze drifted around the room, noticing more nautical decor I would probably purchase for my own room if I had the space or money. My right arm drifted up above my head, nearing the headboard that was draped in a fine vintage fish net with beautiful seashells scattered about. I traced one of the seashells with a gentle hand. The pendant light hanging off to the side of the bed was made from an antique glass fishing float. My dad had found some of these Japanese hand-blown glass fishing floats on the shores of northern California a long time ago. This one still had the original net.

I should take a picture of it and text it to Dad.

Between the fish net wrapped around the headboard and the fishing glass pendant was a unique dream catcher dangling from a small hook on the wall. My hand stretched out as I reached for it, then slid lightly over the sea star embedded into the decorative bottom half of the dream catcher. As I lightly ran my finger over the star, I wondered if Floridians called them sea stars or starfish. Slowly, I ran my hand up to the dream catcher's center weaving, feeling its fragile state.

So this is where all my dreams have gone.

Well rested and wondering what the day would bring, I pushed off the sheets and floated toward the bathroom, where I noticed a sign off to the side of the door that read, The Poop Deck.

They have a sense of humor, I see.

The nautical term for the loo or bathroom was the head. The poop deck was the covered cabin at the back of a ship, or the aft observing cabin. Sailors must have had a sense of humor too.

After my shower, I hung my towel on the boat cleat attached to the wall next to the shower, then propped the bathroom door open with the painted buoy door stop. After dressing, I found my way downstairs to make a cup of coffee. The smell alone was blissful.

Gazing out the glass sliding doors from the kitchen area, I could see Jessica in the pool, floating on a pool raft that was more of a sofa. It had a backrest and pillows, with drink holders on both ends. Glancing around the room and into the den and office, I saw that Mr. Jones was nowhere in sight. Looking back toward the pool, I smiled at how content Jessica seemed floating.

Drawing a heart with Reddi-wip to top off my coffee, I took a sip before heading outside. As I reached for the door handle, a soft tingling sensation ran through my body. It was like a feeling of home, amity, and comfort. I pried my gaze up from the task at hand and looked back toward the other end of the kitchen where I sensed someone was standing. Sure enough, there stood a young man, maybe thirty, with sandy-colored, uncombed hair. His tall, lean frame gave him a sporty look, like he could be a professional athlete in any sport. His deep-brown eyes stared my way confidently, and there was a moment. He took my breath away, and I felt lightheaded. Our gaze lingered too long for strangers.

The eyes are the window to the soul. In thought, I pulled my gaze from his and looked back down at my coffee cup, counted to three, and dared myself to look back up and introduce myself.

But he was gone.

My feet guided me toward the area where he'd been standing, but then I heard the front door open and shut. I tried to take in a deep breath, but it felt like someone had sucker punched me in the gut.

Why didn't I say anything? Why did I look away? What is wrong with me?!

The tingling feeling, the goosebumps, had vanished with him. Suddenly, my feet felt heavy and ached painfully, and I had the urge to moan. It took everything I had to move from where he once stood. Slowly the pain subsided and my breathing returned to normal, so I turned to walk outside and join Jessica at the pool. When I grabbed for the doorknob, I heard buzzing sounds from above me.

Mr. Jones's alarm is going off again. Maybe I will leave him a note later. That buzzing and beeping could wake the whole neighborhood!

As I walked away, the sounds faded into nothing. Outside, the sun was shining, and the temperature was somewhere between unreal and marvelous again. I almost started wondering where the hot Florida weather was hiding but didn't want to jinx perfection.

This is why everyone spring breaks in Florida!

"Another superb day here in Florida!" Jessica said as if she were going to make a report on the weather channel. But she didn't go on. Something had made her stop. Her expression went blank.

I waited for her to say more, then decided to try following her gaze out toward the lake. I asked her, "What are you staring at?"

I glanced back out toward the lake, looking for a gator, thinking maybe that's what had her attention. Her gaze turned to me, then she held her hand out to me. I held her hand for a moment, and she smiled and said, "Everything is going to be okay. I love you, Rose!"

Then I replied, "Ditto, Jess!" I wondered where this had come from as she let go of my hand and her expression changed back to her normal, high-spirited self.

Oh no! I thought. *Did she get her midterm exam grades and they weren't as good as she thought they would be? With that thought, I don't care to know what my midterm exam grades are,* I lied to myself, then ran my necklace back and forth between my fingers.

"It's a glorious day! Let's live life like we have never lived before," she said as she flipped her hair, laughed, and patted the empty place next to her on the oversized float.

I put my coffee down on the ledge of the pool and jumped, with no idea what possessed me to do it. Maybe I just wanted to lighten the mood. When I landed on the float, Jessica flew as if floating on air before her grand entrance into the pool. Who knew my little framed body would toss her up that high? We laughed, even snorted, and when we could control our bodies again from the hysterics, I held out my hand to give her a lift back on the raft and she pulled me into the water with her. Since sixth grade, we could do absolutely anything together and laugh until we cried. That moment had been no different!

After hours in the pool, Mr. Jones showed us how to pick a ripe pineapple and slice it into a piece of art. With the time spent, it was hard seeing the slices disappear, but they truly tasted spectacular. After we helped him water the garden using the house's graywater, he showed us how the water was collected and basically recycled for this task. For lunch, he helped us find the best avocados on the tree and had us place them on a table, where a few had sat for about the past two weeks to ripen enough to eat. I had no idea a fresh avocado tasted so good and learned a new trick about how to ripen them. Plant to table. Who knew I would think every bite was a slice of heaven? I could only wonder what delicious meal would be created next.

Dear Journal,

Tomorrow…maybe we will meet the young man Mr. Jones told us was staying here. This morning I heard a noise, and when I glanced up, I saw him walk out the front door. Although we've never met, every time I think of him or catch a glance of him, a tingle runs around my body, I quiver, and my heart skips a beat. I don't know why, but for some reason, I feel we need to meet—but why? I've never felt this way and would rather be dragged across the horse arena by my stirrup than meet a stranger, but he made me feel different. Different—I don't know how.

I plan on visiting the library room to see what books I might want to read. The library is near the front door, and maybe he will come back and I will be looking for a book and accidentally we will meet. Even if I don't see this mystery man, my goal is to find a short and sweet book to read. I would enjoy some time with a book that is not on a class syllabus.

Reading a book out on the dock sounds like the thing to do, but Jessica just asked if I would like to join her for s'mores out at the firepit. I cannot lie…I am hoping *mystery man* will join us. I at least want to see him again. I have never felt that way around anyone—ever! Why does my skin tingle?

Feeling: Inquisitive, but not a nosy Rose.

CHAPTER 5

AN OCEAN WAVE

Monday, 29th of March

Dear Journal,

It must be past midnight now. I was awakened by a dream I had, the kind you don't think you will ever forget, but in the morning, you wake and can't remember one thing, only the way it made you feel. My heart was beating hard inside my chest. It didn't seem to race, but I noticed it thumping almost as if I was lightly being hit. Matter of fact, it was the only thing I felt. A light off in the distance slowly neared. A train maybe—I was on train tracks. Then I felt his hand, and even in the dark, I knew it was a man, his hand strong and warm as he held my slight hand in his. I felt weak—a jittery feeling—and could feel my hands cool and become clammy in his. Then he gently let go of my hand and caressed my cheek. My body felt limp—no, maybe light as a feather.

There was no doubt I had never felt this way before. The question was, who was this man? Why was a light coming my way? In fear of the light, I woke! Why? Now, more than anything, I want to feel that combination of strange emotions again. I must be brave and come out of my shell, put myself out there for a life that's open to feeling, especially what I felt as the man caressed my cheek.

Maybe the dream happened because my thoughts are on the man I've never met…and no, he didn't show up at the firepit last night, but I've been listening for a car and the front door chimes.

Feeling: A Rose thirsting to bloom.

A PHONE RANG SOMEWHERE WITHIN the house, and a faint beeping sound pulsed under the sounds of several hurried footsteps off in the distance. I rolled over in bed and adjusted my new favorite pillow. My head felt as if it was resting on a cloud as I fell in and out of sleep. The light drawn into the room danced on an ocean wave. The wave was a beautiful glass vase that sat empty on one of the shelves across the room. I thought of the white roses and gardenias in the front yard and how their clippings would be beautiful in that vase. Those were my favorite two flowers in the world, and they smelled heavenly.

My eyes drifted over to the dream catcher. *You didn't catch all my dreams? I'm glad, but I wish you could tell me about the young man in the dream!*

I heard echoing footsteps and realized people were walking outside my room. They were talking, whispering. I wasn't sure if I liked the partial dream left in my head to wrestle with all day, but something told me to leave it alone. If it was love I'd dreamed about, it would come when the timing was right and not before I was ready. I found myself feeling for my necklace and tugged at it to make sure it was there.

When I have the courage to form words, a complete sentence or two would be nice. For now, I should enjoy my vacation.

The lingering smell of coffee convinced me to toss the covers off and break out for the adventure that the day had in store for me. As I dressed, I heard voices, a conversation I couldn't make sense of but nor was it any of my business. Stepping outside my room, I half expected to see people standing around talking, but no one was around. I must have just heard a television on somewhere. I heard laughing coming from the kitchen and followed the self-confident voice, the familiar flair that is Jessica.

"Look at these beautiful tomatoes," she said with such wonder and amazement as she held one up to her nose and breathed in the scent. "Who knew they would smell so amazing home grown?"

I'm wondering if she ever smelled a tomato before now.

"Just wait until you taste them, but you will have to wait for dinner," Mr. Jones said as he submersed the whole bowl of tomatoes in a pot of water on the stove. "Would you like to help make homemade pasta tonight? It's really easy. Basically, it's an egg, a little water and flour, and the pasta-making machine does the hard work for us." Mr. Jones smiled at us and turned his attention to the pot of tomatoes he was preparing to skin.

Jessica smiled at me, knowing this was one of my favorite meals. Then she replied for us both, "Yes, please!"

"I would love to help with the sauce too, if that is okay with you?" I said to Mr. Jones.

"Of course! But don't you two want to go enjoy

the lake today? The kayaks are ready for you," Mr. Jones replied with a nod toward the dock. "Don't forget the binoculars. You never know what you might see out there."

"Wait! I need to get my phone and a hat," I said as I scurried to my room.

Mr. Jones smiled when I returned to the kitchen and asked, "Do you plan on calling someone while out on the lake?"

"My phone is the only way I can document this experience for us, plus I want a picture of an alligator too. Well, from a distance anyway," I said, giggling but knowing I was terrified of the unknown, like a gator.

Jessica and I chose the kayak for two, then walked it down the dock toward the beach and lowered it into the clear, tea-colored water. The lake was like glass. Not a ripple, no wind, just sunshine from above. Jessica walked back to grab the two paddles as I took my seat in the back of the kayak.

It's safer in the kayak—a little harder for an alligator to pull me under the water. It's funny how sharks didn't seem to bother me while living on the sailboat, but a gator...to me, that's an unfamiliar beast.

As Jessica stepped off the steps and into the lake, she used the end of a paddle to splash me with the chilly water. The shock was real, but we giggled. She then stepped into the kayak as if it were a huge yacht and, before I could say a word, she flipped us out of the kayak and into the water. Jessica yelped as she arose from the lake, as I did too but for a different reason.

"My phone!"

I quickly dove back in and sifted through the sandy bottom. I saw the rectangular outline of my phone under a thin layer of sand and scooped it up. As I stood there, thankful I'd found it in the sand, I knew it was probably of no use to me any longer. I shook it off and laid it on the dock to dry. Even though I felt the ping of stress over the loss of my phone, I couldn't contain my laughter when the memory of our yelps danced back in my mind.

"I wish that was on video!" I laughed.

"Me too!" Jessica replied.

The second attempt at getting in the kayak was successful, and we made our way out to explore Lake Minnehaha. Drifting, moving freely, not a care in the world. We took in the warmth of the sun as it dried our suits, while listening to the water softly slap against the kayak hull. The birds chirped, followed by the splashing of a frog or two diving off their safe lily pads, and there was the occasional fly-by from a dragonfly or two as we made our way around the shoreline. Several Sandhill Cranes flew over us, talking loudly to one another.

"Those are the birds that were making so much noise in the neighbors' yard, when, suddenly, I saw the neighbor lady run outside and chase them away," Jessica said with a laugh.

Pointing up at the eagle, I said, "That looks like a bald eagle but with a different pattern of white. What is that bird?"

"It's an Osprey," she replied as a matter of fact.

I lifted my eyebrow in question. "And you know this how?"

"Mr. Jones!" she said, laughing at how much he had taught her in the short while we'd been there. Then she added, "He said these huge birds have nests at the top of the cypress trees just around the corner from the house. They fly hovering high above the water and dive in fishing for food, and sometimes they even land in his backyard."

We floated and paddled everywhere in hopes of spotting a gator, and even though we were unsuccessful, we were pretty sure they spotted us. It was hours before we returned to Mr. Jones's dock with our share of stories to tell.

I reached for my phone and the screen was black, so I tapped it, hoping it would wake. But no…it was a goner. *RIP, old friend. I'd hoped you would have survived a little plunge into the lake.*

"Jess, when you think about it, can you text my parents and tell them my phone took a dip in Lake Minnehaha and didn't survive?" I said as I held up my phone.

"Sure! My phone is in my bedroom. It's been so

nice being unplugged. I am not sure it's charged," she answered as Mr. Jones approached the dock.

"Did you see any alligators today?" he asked as he helped us lift the kayak out of the water and place it back on the dock.

"Nope, but we did see some huge turtles and I managed to kill a phone," I replied.

Mr. Jones met my gaze with a smile and said, "Sorry about the phone. Well, I've been cooking something special for you girls." He secured the kayak and turned to lead the way to the house.

I followed him back along the path, then turned to see Jessica staring out at the lake, soaking up the moment and listening to the birds above.

"I am about to add my special secret seasoning to the sauce. I have to ask first, is a dab of fire in your food okay with you and Jessica?" Mr. Jones asked.

I answered with a nod and said, "Spice a dish with hot love and it pleases every palate!"

Mr. Jones let out a huge bellowing laugh and said, "I said that to my wife every time we cooked together."

I've never heard that saying before. Here I thought I just made it up.

"How I loved hot, spicy food. She, on the other hand, wasn't as much of a fan," he added.

We laughed as we walked into the kitchen. He took the lid off the pot, and we both took in the rich smells. He placed the lid back on, and I watched as he pulled his "secret" spice from the spice rack, tucked away in the back with a few other spices that looked like they'd been purchased from a store. But I knew he had reused the jars for his own garden blends.

"It is a secret because I didn't grow this here. Don't tell anyone," Mr. Jones whispered as if someone from his life was going to shame him for purchasing spices from the store.

"The label is peeled off. What is it?" I asked, now more curious than before.

"Tell no one," he said as his eyes met mine and waited for my answer.

"I promise!" I replied quickly, wondering who I would ever tell and if I would ever find that person I could cook and create memories with like he had with Mrs. Jones.

"It's a blend of four peppers, premium red chili flakes, habanero, jalapeño, and the little extra kick is the ghost peppers! Sure, you can use any paprika or red pepper blend, but this mix adds that special kick. But not too much to set your guests on fire!" he said, smiling ear to ear.

He sprinkled a dash here and there, then took the long wooden spoon and slowly stirred it in. He waved his cupped hand over the pot in his direction and took in the aroma. "It will take a few hours for the spices to work their magic." He replaced the lid on the large pot and made sure the stove heat was on low. "We will start making pasta in about an hour or two. Whenever you and Jessica want," he said as he turned to wash his hands.

I took that as my cue to go find Jessica.

I wanted to ask him about the other guest, but what would I say? My face warmed as another image of the man swam through my thoughts. Then I remembered how I saw him but was too dumbfounded to say a word. Never would I have the courage to ask. I could only make fun of how I would ask Mr. Jones. Hey, I was curious about the hot guy staying here? Oh, and I can't stop thinking of him and he visits me in my dreams nightly. My face glistened, and I needed to find Jessica, but first I needed to cool my face before she saw me blushing.

It was so quiet in the house. No footsteps. No television. Well, until I heard someone weeping and sniffling. I followed the cry and peeked my head around the corner near the library. Jessica's hair was backlit from the afternoon sun that danced through the window, giving her the most beautiful glow as she sat in the reading chair near the tall bookshelf.

Is Jess crying? I wondered as I inched my way closer.

From where I stood, I couldn't see Jessica's face, but my attention was drawn to the dark maple wood sliding ladder that reached all the way to the top shelf. I wondered how anyone could keep small kids and the elderly from climbing up the two-story ladder and getting hurt. A wave of sorrow washed over me like an ocean wave receding, being sucked back out to sea. I closed my eyes, took a deep breath, opened my eyes, and slowly processed my feelings. Then I took a few steps closer and whispered, "Jess."

She held up her index finger to her lips as another whimper came from the adjoining room, the music room. I slipped around the corner to get closer to Jessica, wondering again who was crying.

"She's so sad. Rose, promise me you will never be this sad," Jessica said as I realized she was sitting just out of sight from Mrs. Jones.

"Okay, I promise. Are you watching Mrs. Jones cry?" I asked, slightly troubled at my allegation.

"No!" she whispered, her hands wrapping tighter around a book. When she noticed my glance, she loosened her grip and held the book out and said, "I think you might like this one."

The sailboat on the cover caught my eye, and I studied it for a moment and then read the title, *Girl Sailing Aboard the Western Star.* The back cover read, "Annie makes new friends despite her painful shyness. Will experiencing amazing new adventures and discovering a whole new world above and below the deep blue sea help Annie be ready for whatever her future as a teenager brings?" Sailing, girl journaling, true story, 214 pages long, a short read—Jess knew me well.

"Yes, I would like to read this. Thank you for

finding this book for me. Maybe I will relive my younger days living on a sailboat." I whispered to Jessica when chills suddenly ran up and down my arms, "Let's go outside. The vibe in here is too heavy."

We walked in the opposite direction of the music room, and I stopped to observe the raised little hairs on my arms stand straight to attention, my feet stopped moving and some sort of fear washed over me. Concentrating on the little details of my surroundings, I tried to figure out what was causing this feeling, but then the goosebumps settled, and everything went back to normal.

Jessica's long stride glided her past me, and when my legs allowed me to move, I followed her out the door. Leaving the house, I stopped and looked around the pool area and back at the house but saw no one. But was sure someone was watching. The thought of the man, the guest I had not yet met, had sneaked back into my thoughts.

Why would goosebumps running up and down my body bring visions of a certain hunky man into my thoughts?

"Are you coming?" Jessica said when she noticed I had stopped following her.

I nodded and followed her along the path. The scent of lemongrass eased my mind until I had that feeling again, someone was watching. I paused, slowing my steps to look back. Again, nothing! I quickened my stride to join Jessica near the lake's sandy shoreline. She was already removing her shirt and shorts, revealing a cute new swimsuit, then she chose one of two lounge chairs placed on the small beach at the lake's edge and, graceful as a butterfly, sat down to bask in the late afternoon sun.

As I settled down in the lounge chair beside her, I looked out across the lake and said, "If only I wasn't afraid of alligators, we could sun and swim here."

"No alligators will get you here," Jessica replied.

No gators, said only people who aren't afraid of anything!

"What an incredible place." Jessica smiled and slid her sunglasses on as she looked out across the lake. "My whole life, I've never been so content and at peace as I am right now. It's a little piece of heaven!"

Dear Journal,

The days are drifting away as Jessica and I recharge our internal batteries here on Lake Minnehaha. No fuss, simply content with doing very little, and yet our days are filled with unique adventures. Even the modest chores we offer to do around the house seem effortless and really satisfying. Watering the garden's reward is taking in the fragrance and knowing later we will pick the fruit of our labor by enjoying a snack or a meal.

Tandem kayaking has been a daily self-guided tour around the lake. We've heard and watched as Egrets and Ospreys fish and hunt for meals. Ducks swim past as if we don't exist, so very bravely—I could take a note or two from them. We saw an alligator lounged on the shoreline of the vacant lots where no homes have been built, and it wasn't as scary as I thought it would be.

Mr. Jones showed us some photography tips and tricks with his film camera and showed us photographs he's taken throughout his life. He could open his own gallery, and when I told him that, he only nodded his head. I felt a glimpse of sorrow and realized I didn't think before I spoke. Maybe he had tried and it hadn't succeeded, but with his talent,

I can't believe that would be the case. I feel more comfortable talking with him. He has shared things with me I will never forget.

I learned how to make homemade pasta and sauce. It was as easier than I had ever imagined.

I even found time to read a few chapters of *Girl Sailing the Western Star* by the campfire's light. I am enjoying the book—it practically reads itself. It was lucky that Jessica stumbled across it for me.

There is one thing happening that is strange. I feel like I am remembering a dream, or maybe a daydream, but only bits of it are coming to me. It's about a boy, a man, and he makes me feel like nothing I've ever felt before. It makes me regret not having a boyfriend. Well, never dating at all! The feeling of wanting more life experiences, like the life that Mr. and Mrs. Jones have here, and the love I feel in this house, I want it too. I know I am young, but it makes me sad. I am mourning a life I haven't yet lived, but how do I swim with the gators when I am too frightened to get my feet wet? Never mind. I would not swim with the gators, but how do I get over the fact that I can't move, or speak, when a handsome man *might* be near? I've not yet met him, but he visits me while I sleep. It seems I am more open-minded and ready for the world. Well, one tiny baby step at a time, and I realize I must be awake to truly experience it!

Feeling: Rose, it's time to open my eyes.

CHAPTER 6

DÉJÀ VU

Tuesday, 30ᵗʰ of March

"**S**HHHH," JESSICA SAID THROUGH A giggle. We slid through the sliding door, entering the house from the back-yard where we couldn't seem to pry ourselves away from the firepit and basking under a blanket of stars.

"Do you think we turned the fire pit off all the way? Did you grab the extra marshmallows that were on the table?" I questioned Jessica, worried about leaving out a mess for Mr. Jones, who had left us after the Disney fireworks show.

I wished the house was a little closer to see the show better, but it was still magical from twenty miles away.

Jessica returned the bag of marshmallows and graham crackers to the pantry while I placed the skewers in the sink to soak the sticky ends.

"I'm off to climb the stairway to my heavenly

room." Jessica smiled, heading toward the staircase as I filled a glass of water before heading up myself.

What a wonderful evening! What a fantastic day. But I'm feeling tired. It's only just past midnight, and I can't wait to sleep.

CLUNK!

I heard a heavy door shutting, but where? I hadn't remembered any door that heavy in this house to sound like that. My mind raced, and my heart fluttered in my chest.

Maybe someone dropped something.

I ran my necklace between my fingers and looked around. Nothing else seemed out of place, and the house fell silent again. As I climbed the steps, I slowed, then paused and looked back over my shoulder. I felt someone nearby.

It's probably Jess. She's in the next room!

I slipped into my room and shut and locked the door. Looking at my bed, I felt my body grow heavy with a sense of fatigue, and my mouth was dry. I took a sip of my water and couldn't wait to crash into bed.

Before I knew it, I heard the familiar *tap, rap, tap, tap, tap*—our code knock. Jessica was knocking at my bedroom door, then she slid through the door like an angel, danced across the floor, grabbed my swimsuit from the whale tail hook just inside the bathroom, and tossed it on top of me. I couldn't help but smile at her, even though I could have slept for another hour or two.

"Good morning! Let's go to the beach!" She smiled and spun away, paused at the Wyland *Sea Turtle Shipwreck* print hanging on the wall, and said, "Isn't this one of your favorite Wyland prints?"

I smiled back at her and nodded, offering her affirmation, and said, "This nautical room reminds me of all the things in the world not yet explored."

"Or does it remind you of all the things you have not yet explored?" She winked at me, smiled and walked out, closing the door behind her. Then her voice sang out, "I'll meet you in the car in five."

Sliding out of bed, I felt stiff, as if I hadn't moved in days, but I shook it off and readied for today's adventure. *A new adventure, a new day! I will have confidence and not be as shy as I was even yesterday. A new daily affirmation?!* I thought as I grabbed my packed day bag and admired the print on the wall for another moment. It had been years since we flew to Hawaii for a family wedding where I saw the two whale murals at the Kauai Village shopping center. I remembered reading about these Wyland Whaling Walls and that he traveled basically around the world painting murals. Those huge masterpieces quickly became the highlight of our family Hawaiian vacation. After, I had read everything I could find about the artist and soon became a fan of all art, especially Wyland's underwater paintings and other artists focusing on ocean scenes and lighthouses. At the sight of Wyland's print, I felt the need to force my breath in and out of my lungs.

Wyland's art simply takes my breath away!

As I forced air in and then exhaled, I felt my day bag heavy in my hand, reminding me that Jessica was waiting in the car.

Yes, we are going to the beach!

My free hand pulled the bedroom door open, but I noticed roses and gardenias in the wave vase sitting on the shelf and paused to inhale their sweet fragrance. Only Jessica could have snuck those flowers in there. Another perfect morning for her. She was on cloud nine at this place. I figured it might be difficult getting her to go back to school after being here.

Leaving the house for the first time from the front door, I paused and glanced around, trying to recall the day we arrived. My hand reached for the doorknob, but before I gripped it, I allowed my finger to feel the renaissance pattern throughout the knob and hardware plate. A prickle ran through my arm, causing me to jerk my hand away. I watched as the door slowly pushed open. Taking a step backward, I wondered who was opening the door. My gaze moved from the doorknob and up the muscular forearm, to the broad chest, and landed once again in the deepest warm brown eyes I had ever seen. They had a hint of copper flecks around the edges, making them almost sparkle. Time stood still, my body numb and my mouth dry.

Why am I so thirsty?

My eyes never wavered from his. He cleared his throat, and I hoped he would say the first words because once again, I had nothing. He mumbled something I couldn't understand. I reached for the words or even a "what," but nothing came out, and then he dashed inside the house.

What?! I thought we had a moment. But he didn't say a word to me, just a muddle of jumbled words. And then I couldn't move and found myself once more saying nothing at all.

There was a strong sense of familiarity in his gaze, although we had never met before—*and still haven't!* A strong jamais vu moment—the opposite of déjà vu. I stood motionless in front of the door, staring. This door was so oddly unfamiliar, though I knew I'd have entered through this door the day we arrived. That day was so foggy though, because I'd been so tired.

I should ask Jess why she left me in the car alone that day. That was terrifying.

In the driveway, I saw Jessica sitting in her car, smiling in my direction. She had already put the convertible top down and was sliding her dark sunglasses on.

I put the bizarre feeling and memories aside and jumped into her little red convertible. "Ready!" I said as I plopped myself down in the passenger seat. "Did you meet the guy who is renting the room on the first floor?" I asked.

She replied with a shake of her head, and her hair flew back into movie star position as we sped away from the house. Pleased with myself, I had wrestled and successfully put my hair up before I left my room.

"Let's go experience life on the beach!" Jessica said before she turned up the stereo volume, then raised her hand up in the air and let it float over her head, swaying to the beat of the classic Led Zeppelin song, "Stairway to Heaven." She grinned, even with her eyes, while soaking up every word sung as if the lyrics were being absorbed through her skin, making a place in her soul.

I joined in on the chorus, "Ooh, makes me wonder."

We didn't turn east toward the popular spring break spot, Cocoa Beach. Instead, we headed the opposite direction and landed on the Gulf side in a community called Anna Maria Island where we could rent bikes, golf carts, or do just about anything under the sun. There were beaches and a farmers' market, stores, and a trolley car. We could schedule a session to make arts and crafts, like creating our very own handmade wooden signs, or go shopping in dozens of boutique shops along the main street. This little town was filled with excitement, yet as calming as writing messages in the sand.

The soft white sand flowed through my toes as I sat off the side of the classy lounger in our rented beach suite, which included two cushioned lounge chairs, a canopy shade, and a small table with snacks and drinks.

"How did you pay for this beach suite, Jessica?" I asked, concerned about my share.

"Mom and Dad treated us. They said I could treat you to something nice, and well, this is something nice!" Jessica replied, smiling as she peeked over her sunglasses rim and met my curious gaze.

"You amaze me, Jess!" I smiled at her and felt a ping of guilt, but Jessica did what Jessica wanted, and this was too perfect to argue over.

The seagulls flew overhead in search of a free meal, soon scoring a fry from some unexpecting child, and then several squawked in a frenzy of hope that they too could feast on a greasy potato stick. A short distance from shore, a small fishing boat, maybe a seventeen-foot Boston Whaler, moved at trolling speed, causing a large wake. The onlookers watched as dolphins jumped through the boat's wake. I could only hope the captain was aware of the manatees that lived nearby.

There must be laws about the manatees that all boaters know. I hope!

We walked along the beach and saw spectacular

sand sculptures being created by a group of sand sculpture artists. My heart thumped in my chest and quickened at the sight and being in the mix of all the people, but I stopped anyway. The artists' hands quickly moved along the sand, transforming millions of grains of white sand into a gigantic manatee with her calf beside her, munching on seagrass. The details were impressive. A tingly sensation ran underneath my hair, around my neck, causing goosebumps to flush over my face and even my ears as it had back at the lake house. I rotated my head slowly around in a circular motion and placed my hands behind my neck, but I couldn't control the urge. I quivered. My heart pounded in my ears, and I felt it race even faster inside my chest. As I looked around, I felt a strong sense of something, maybe someone, very familiar, but who? I held a necklace link between two fingers as the crowd began to feel as if they were hovering over me instead of the amazing sand sculptures. My body shook as I stepped farther away, and everything seemed quiet again.

Wow! That was an intense déjà vu moment!

A few yards away, Jessica held up two pairs of masks and snorkels to get my attention, and I joined her at the water's edge.

"Where did you find these?" I asked as I dipped them down in the salty water to rub them clean.

"The beach valet had them for us. Isn't it a picture-perfect place for a swim and a snorkel?" Jessica said. She walked slowly into the water and filled the mask up with ocean water and then rubbed her fingers inside, cleaning the lenses off as she gracefully walked farther into the ocean. We both were PADI certified scuba divers, but never before had we snorkeled or scuba dove together.

Smiling, I playfully splashed as I stepped deeper into the water. I followed her while adjusting the strap on my mask, feeling the Gulf's saltwater felt nice around my legs. It brought memories to the forefront of my mind of the million times I'd snorkeled with my mom and dad off the boat. We would snorkel for pleasure and to find or catch our next meal. I dunked my head under the water to wet my hair and then slipped the mask on, adjusted my snorkel, and joined Jessica, who had already floated a few yards ahead of me. Once I caught up, we watched the scenic view change with every slow, long kick our legs made. The sandy shoreline evolved to small coral banks with tropical fish darting here and there. We found patches of seagrass where, out of nowhere, a magnificent sea turtle curiously swam by. I felt the urge to feel for my gold necklace ship chain I'd had since my ninth birthday because I didn't feel its usual weight in the weightlessness of being underwater. My left-hand fingers found the chain and glided over its smooth surface, more memories flooded in, and I remembered when scuba diving, I would take off the chain because I didn't want any fish to be attracted to the shiny links and think it was something for them to eat.

Jessica pointed toward the sandy bottom, then dove down about eighteen, maybe twenty feet. Graceful as a mermaid, she skimmed the sandy ocean floor and made her way back holding a conch shell in her hand. It felt like she was under the water for too many minutes. Even I, as an experienced free diver, would be too wary to stay down that long. Although, it had been years, so maybe I had held my breath for that long or it just seemed so long because I was watching instead of the one doing it, and as I grew older, it seemed I worried over just about everything. Unlike how it was when I lived on the boat—nothing seemed to bother me, but life was different. We didn't see many people, and when we did, it wasn't me who had to do any of the talking.

When Jessica broke through the surface, she removed her snorkel and said, "It's empty. No one is home. Do you want to keep it?"

I removed my snorkel and spit salt water out of my mouth, relieving the taste of salty hard plastic and silicone. "It would be a great addition to the shell collection, or we could add it to the fish net decor in the nautical room I am staying in," I replied as I inspected the conch shell closer, knowing those creatures hide deep inside and if you take a shell out of water while they are hiding back in their home, they die and stink like no other stench in the world.

Jessica smiled and swam a little farther down the shoreline, with me in tow. We were near the seagrass. I was sure Jessica hoped to find some dolphins or manatees to swim alongside.

Although illegal, it's every Florida tourist's dream!

No such luck finding any yet, but we did find some tropical fish trying to get a better glimpse of us while darting back and forth between the rocks and vegetation. There were sea stars and sand dollars, plus a very curious tiny octopus caught our attention and then swished and meandered away. We smiled at one another, and laughter vibrated out through our snorkels. Before long we swam up along the beach where we got in, and I was happy to see fewer people gathered around the sand sculptures. I felt more comfortable to take another look.

We returned the masks and snorkels to the valet and then walked the shoreline. We passed the completed sand sculptures, some already losing their structure as families posed too close for pictures. Children ran from one sculpture to the next, finding their favorite one and causing more destruction, but everyone was so excited and enjoying the event that it didn't seem to matter. The family was so involved, having fun and taking pictures, they didn't seem to be bothered by any other person around. Which made it nice for me, because I didn't feel the pressure to say anything. We simply walked past them.

We sat on the lounge chairs and laughed about the sea horses and tiny octopuses swimming up to us. Jessica's gaze turned toward the water, and my mind slipped back to an unfamiliar place, a man who I had never met. As if an unknown scent triggered my thoughts and then my imagination would run toward him, leaving me no choice but to follow. His tall, lean body…I could picture him being an Olympic swimmer. No, maybe a baseball player. I shook my head as if to shake away the burning sensation I felt rush up my neck and fill my cheeks. I grabbed my sunscreen and reapplied it, to fend off the sunburn, but I knew better. This wasn't sun—it was blood warmed from my thoughts.

Jessica broke the silence. "Let's go paddleboard!"

I replaced the lid on my sunscreen and noticed Jessica didn't wait for a response. We were going! I trotted down toward the shoreline where the boards were and listened as Jessica spoke to the valet. She handed me a paddle and pointed to the board with a beautiful dolphin painted on the top. She grabbed the one with the sea horse and then asked if I was okay with that one or we could trade. I had never paddleboarded before and had no preference with the artwork, so I grabbed the board and took it into the water. Jessica stood on the board with ease, so not knowing any different, I went to stand and quickly found myself back in the water with a big splash.

Jessica laughed. "It takes a minute to get used to balancing."

"Oh, thanks!" I responded with a playful glare and smacked the top of the water with my hand, splashing her.

My body shook, so the board mimicked my movements and tossed me once more.

"This board is defective, I think!" I shouted to Jessica as she gracefully drifted around me, still laughing.

It took me a couple more times and a few deep breaths, and then when I stood, I wasn't holding the paddle. Tears streamed out of Jessica's eyes as she fell off the board, laughing. She swam over to my paddle and handed it up to me, gracefully stood up on her board, and we slowly made our way, paddling around for hours, enjoying the water from a different point of view. We ventured off, floating, drifting, and paddling along the shore and near the seagrass and found a mother manatee and her calf. We kept our distance and enjoyed watching them graze and frolic along the bed of seagrass. Oh, hence the nickname, sea cows. Watching them eat made my stomach grumble.

"Are you hungry, Rose?" Jessica said with a raised eyebrow toward my stomach.

"I guess so!" I laughed.

We headed back to our suite and ate conch fritters and drank coconut milk and watched a fisherman feed his leftover fish bait to some very happy pelicans. Then we rode the town trolley up and down Main Street and shared a slice of homemade key lime pie. What a wonderful little island to visit. I never wanted to forget this place.

We then gathered our belongings from our suite, including the beautiful conch shell, and stepped toward the water again to take in one last look together before leaving. We looked out over the water as the sun began to set.

"Breathtaking!" I said with a sigh but felt an odd sensation, almost memory-like, of me standing right there, right then but with the man I'd never met. I felt a warm and safe feeling rush over me, not the awkward, jittery and unable to speak feeling I typically had when near or even thinking of a man.

"What a notable day!" Jessica said with a glow of contentment as the warm colors from the horizon's setting sun danced across the ocean. Her comment shook my thoughts away from standing with the man I didn't know, and I nodded my head in agreement.

We leisurely made our way back to the lake house with the top down, the wind blowing through our hair, and our hearts beating to music, as we reminisced about another perfect day.

Dear Journal,

Today Jessica and I snorkeled and learned a new kind of floating. We paddleboarded! Off the beaches of Anna Maria Island. Jessica took to the paddleboard like a bird to flight, but I was a little more like a puffin trying to take off out of the ocean, flapping like crazy until it finally happened. Once the fear was gone, I stood and balanced, then I didn't want to stop. I am not sure what the fear was, but it had a hold of me and then seemed to set like the sun and disappear.

This day trip was one of my favorite highlights of Florida, and it's official, I love manatees as much as sea turtles, and that's saying something! I felt more love today than ever in my life, but I am not sure how to explain it or even why the feeling of love was in the mix.

When Jessica wouldn't let me pay for anything today, I knew instantly she'd already taken care of it with her parents' help. Her family has always looked out for me, made sure I was included and without making me feel uncomfortable. This is one of the many things I love about her and why I call her mom and dad, Mom and Dad #2. How can I ever thank them enough for this magical day?!

I am living in island time. I don't have my watch on, but guess what…I don't care! It seems everything works out just perfectly no matter what we do, what adventure we take, or where we go. Time just doesn't matter here, and it's quite possible I have lost my everyday worries. It feels like a huge weight has been lifted from me.

Feeling: Don't worry about a thing…'cause every little Rose is gonna be all right.

CHAPTER 7

THE WIND IN OUR SAILS

Wednesday, 31ˢᵗ of March

CLANK, CLUNK, PING, SQUISH. CLANK, *clunk, ping, squish.*

Slowly my eyes opened, and *I looked toward the single beam of light that was trying to break through the edge of the full blackout shades in the bedroom window.*

Clank, clunk, ping. The sound grew, and so did my curiosity.

Where were these sounds coming from?

I tossed my sheets off my legs, stretched, and stumbled my way over to the gap, exposing the flicker of light dancing its way in from outside. I placed my hand on the blinds, preparing to squint out into the sunshine, but my gaze landed on a small glass sculpture of two sailboats sailing in opposite directions. My finger slid over the smooth form, and I read what was etched into the base. "Two Ships

That Pass in the Night." In fine print underneath that phrase, it read, "Only you, alone, can choose the direction you want to sail."

I held the delicate creation in my hands, carried it over to the dresser, and placed it in a more secure location. *Who would place a fragile piece of art like this on the ledge of a window?*

Feeling my soothing gold ship chain necklace with my fingers, I thought about where I might have heard this saying before. I wondered if it meant passing someone for a few seconds, or much longer. Did they see one another or not? Is it a stranger, or is it someone who you get to know for years but later disappears in the darkness, like what was happening to old high school friends? However, the small print reminded us that we could change directions if we didn't like what we were doing. Wasn't it? It dawned on me that these were the type of questions that could be brought up in a future psychology class. Then I quickly dismissed everything because they were linked with school.

There will be none of that. I am on vacation!

On the floor I noticed *Girl Sailing Aboard the Western Star*, the book I was reading last night prior to falling asleep. I picked it up and placed it on the bedside table, then paused to thank the dream catcher for catching my dreams again. I wondered if reading about sailing and being in a nautical room…well, maybe I imagined or slightly dreamed the clanking sounds. The clank and clink sounds were similar to those you would hear coming from halyard lines smacking the side of an aluminum sailboat mast.

That makes sense, I guess.

Jessica's giggle spilled over the house and floated up to my room from the kitchen. I twisted my hair back in a French braid and put on my most comfortable shorts with matching top, ready for whatever the day had to offer. A *clank, clunk, ping, squish* noise was followed by another Jessica giggle. I wondered what in the world she was doing. As I rounded the corner to the kitchen, I saw her behind an old-fashioned orange juicer, pulling down the leaver. *Clunk,* the leaver went down. *Crunch* was the sound of the half slice of orange being pressed. And *squish* was the juice flowing out the bottom of the device. *Ping* the juice lever raised back up.

"Good morning! You should taste what I am making," Jessica said, beaming her beautiful smile my way.

"Jessica, don't you mean what our wonderful orange tree produced?" Mr. Jones corrected, followed by a friendly grin.

I grabbed a glass, filled it with the fresh orange juice, and looked down at all the pulp in the glass. As I swallowed and chewed a little, two sets of eyes were upon me.

"Well, what do you think?" Jessica asked as if it was the best thing she'd made in her whole life.

"Well, it's like drink-eating a fresh-squeezed Florida orange," I said with complete honesty.

Both Mr. Jones and Jessica laughed.

"Do you need some help cleaning this mess?" I asked, not wanting to leave a wet, sticky mess for him to clean. *Mom would be proud that I offered.*

Without hesitation, or a reply, I took the garbage can from the bin and was about to slide the dozens of orange halves in when I heard Mr. Jones say, "Oh, wait! If you can, would you please put them in a large bowl for me? I will show you all the ways we use and repurpose these wonderful gifts from nature."

He handed me a large glass bowl and then left Jessica to continue her task as he walked into the pantry and came out with paper towels, sugar, and part of a dehydrator. As he placed them down on the counter, he said, "I will show you the finished products later, but not before I send you and Jessica on an adventure out on the lake."

Jessica and I glanced over at one another, neither of us knowing what he had in mind for us that day.

Mr. Jones placed a string through a couple of the orange halves and said, "Girls, do you mind hanging these out near the bird feeders on the way to the lake? The birds enjoy these citrus treats too!" He handed me the orange slices, and Jessica and I walked outside.

"What do you think Mr. and Mrs. Jones did

before retirement or the B&B?" I asked Jessica as I handed her another orange half to hang.

"They co-owned a water sports store," Jessica said as she hung the fruit. "He told me they used to sell ski boats, jet skis, kayaks, and several other things. They were one of the first Hobie dealers in Florida, and when they sold the shop, they kept several water toys."

"Oh, that explains why they have so many here," I replied.

"After they sold the business, they found themselves in an empty house, so they started their gardens but didn't know what to do next," Jessica said as she stepped off the garden's divider wall. "They loved hosting, so the B&B was a natural step and then they started their new business venture. He said having the water toys attracted more people to their B&B for the right reasons. Rest and relaxation."

We walked toward the dock where we met Mr. Jones standing next to the little thirteen-foot Hobie Wave sailboat. It was rigged and ready to sail, tied near the beach with its yellow-, green-, and orange-striped sail flapping casually in the wind.

"Have either of you sailed before?" Mr. Jones asked.

"I have, but it's been a few years. I lived on a large sailboat when I was little with my family, and we used to get back on the water every summer until I left for college," I replied.

He ran through the basics, handed us two life jackets, and pushed us out away from the beach. The wind gently filled the sail, and we were carried away.

"Have fun, girls! Remember, life is a journey, not a destination," Mr. Jones called out as he snapped a photograph of the two of us sailing away.

"He's right, you know!" Jessica said as she flipped her hair and let it float in the wind. "Every day should be an adventure. If we sit still, it becomes a terminus." She giggled as she reached down and let her fingers glide across the water.

Sailing was a different kind of freedom. It also connected us to Mother Nature in a way few things did, or at least it did for me. I believed the same went for Jess.

The wind took us to the other side of the 2,313-acre lake, where Jessica and I had to execute our first tack—change direction, which means swapping from one side of the boat, crossing the trampoline to the other side while ducking under the sail. This little sailboat was easily manned by one and handled well. I had never sailed a catamaran before. I hadn't known what I was missing, but I knew if I didn't pay attention during the frequent gusts of wind, we could still capsize.

I would rather not swim with the alligators today, or any other day, for that matter.

A few wobbles were had while getting used to being back on the water. Jessica switched from port to starboard side and sat too far off the edge of the starboard hull, and when a gust of wind quickly filled the sail, she almost fell overboard. Somehow, she caught herself, and we sailed onward as we laughed over her flailing moves.

We tacked several more times before it became effortless, and sailing was as easy as the breeze. It was fun to show Jessica how the sail will speak to you and, if you listen, it will tell you something needs to be adjusted. It will flap, signaling the wind changed direction or you steered off course. I showed her how the water would ripple when a gust was moving toward us. We watched the clouds move to help us with wind direction, and I showed her how the little sail monitor would flap horizontally if we had proper sail trim and upward or downward if we needed to pull the sail in or out or turn slightly. Sailing came back to me the moment the occasion arose, like I'd never left the sea.

Jessica crawled her way toward the front on the trampoline and slowly stood upright on the bow. She inched her way, somehow balancing on the main crossbar, leaned against the slender mast, and held on to the forestay bridle, which was the wires holding the mast up. After she found her footing and balanced, she spread her arms out like wings and yelled, "I'm light as a feather and free as a cloud." The wind carried her long blonde hair back to flap against the sail, and she beamed blissfully, looking as if she was prepared to fly.

"If the wind dies and you fall off, it might take me awhile to get back to you!" I said while laughing at the thought but also terrified of not getting back to her before something else did.

After her flight, I watched her inch her way back to the mesh tramp, where our giggles became laughter, our laughter turned to tears, and we fell hopelessly onto the tramp, catching our breaths as we looked up at the sail. Our eyes still watery, everything was a bit blurry. We laid on the trampoline, parallel to the water, and watched the sail above us fill with wind and move us across the water. I rested my feet up on the tiller crossbar and gripped it enough to steer if needed. It almost felt and looked as if we were floating in the clouds instead of across the top of the lake's water. I remember the same feeling on our boat, but that feeling had come from lying under a blanket of stars, not in the light of day. Jessica and I glanced at one another and smiled.

This is pure bliss. What an angelic day!

Dear Journal,

A form of freedom is to let go. We sailed our worries away, letting them fly off into the wind. Well, it was more of a breeze.

I'm still working on letting go of fear. The fear of trying something new and meeting new people. I guess, really, I'm fearful of change. Traveling here with Jessica is a small step toward achieving that goal.

Something new, different, and maybe even life changing.

This trip has given me the courage to explore and be more adventurous. As far as meeting new people, we have made a friend of Mr. Jones, and with all the feelings and thoughts entering my mind, I want to meet the mysterious guest. The man who gives me goosebumps with the mere thought of him. It's as if I am terrified, yet every ounce of me tingles with excitement. This is the first time I've ever *wanted* to meet someone new, especially a man! Maybe it's true that each of our encounters is meant to help us grow. In this case, an encounter would make me *glow*.

When we came in from sailing, Mr. Jones gave us

his homemade candied orange peels, which tasted sweet and sour. He excitedly showed us several things he makes with oranges and orange bits. There was homemade marmalade, which they canned in the cutest mason jars. Other slices of oranges were placed in ice trays. He said that tomorrow we will add those to our drinks to help give them a kick. He used the dehydrating machine and showed us several uses for dried fruit, like kindling in the firepit or fireplace. I had no idea they would repel slugs and could be used to make a citrus vinegar cleaning spray and to clean scorched pots and pans. Ideas that might be helpful when I get my own place. After dinner—which by the way, I tasted the orange zest added to the salad—Mr. Jones shared some of their chocolate-covered treats. Yes, filled with orange peels. I almost declined, but I am glad I changed my mind because they were very tasty. But really, how could I resist chocolate anything?

Mr. Jones is such an interesting gentleman. I'm surprised they don't charge B&B guests more, because of all the extras. He makes turning into an adult a little less scary and a lot more interesting.

Today was another amazing day. Sharing the love of sailing with Jess, and Mr. Jones teaching us new things, sharing some of his cooking knowledge and how to live off the land—at least what's in his gardens. These experiences have made me feel more adult—if that's a thing. I am not the slightest bit uncomfortable. It's even possible they have empowered me.

Feeling: A Rose is more than meets the eye. She just needs the knowledge and courage to drop her petals and make potpourri.

CHAPTER 8

KISSED BY A MANATEE

Thursday, 1ˢᵗ of April

A SOFT, MUFFLED SOUND OF A motor revving, maybe a motorbike, was heard when I rolled over to my side. Pulling the soft pillow closer, I dug my head farther into it, trying to quiet the noise. My pillow made the sound seem muffled as if it were a boat engine I was hearing from under water. I drifted weightlessly in and out of sleep.

Pain ran through my body but pierced my arm the worst. I tried reaching toward the pain, but something stopped me. I tore at my bed sheets, but soon the engine sound faded and I woke. My eyes were now wide open, there was no pain, and I found myself staring at two black-and-white images of manatees cruising around in their habitat. The light softly lingering in the window revealed unique marks along the sea cow's side. Three white marks, gashes, only inches away from one another rounded up to her back. Her pain raced through me as if it were my own pain to possess. An unexpected tear rolled down my cheek and onto my pillow, so I closed my eyes and drifted back into the ocean, into a deep sleep.

Boat propeller cuts!

The room was brighter, and my pillow was damp. I looked up at the dream catcher and remembered the strange but vivid dream. "Was I a manatee?" I questioned no one while running my gold ship chain necklace between my fingers.

The smell of coffee lingered in the air as I held my arm and grimaced from the pain that wasn't there. Leaving the comfort of the bed was hard, but chancing another dream like that one wasn't an option.

As I walked into the kitchen, I noticed an old 2016 *Paddle Tales Newsletter* on the counter. The headline read, "Save the Manatee Club Reaches a Milestone." This was their anniversary newsletter celebrating thirty-five years as a nonprofit organization, or was it thirty-five years of being a club? I thumbed through the magazine, finding myself more curious about the organization and their quest to help save and protect manatees and their aquatic habitat.

"Good morning! I see you've found my favorite nonprofit here in Florida!" Mr. Jones said with pride. He reached over and flipped to a page with a photograph that instantly tugged at my heart. "A manatee's closest relatives are elephants and hyraxes."

What is a hyrax? I know it is a mammal but wish I could look it up. If only my phone hadn't died.

"Manatees average weight is from 800 pounds up to 1200 pounds, but Brutus here"—he pointed at the big huggable creature—"weighs a whopping 1,900 pounds and has been visiting Blue Springs since 1970."

"Mr. and Mrs. Jones have a framed photograph and adoption certificate hanging on the far wall in the study," Jessica said as she casually pointed toward the room beyond the dining room.

"I would love to adopt a manatee. When we get back to school, I'll log on and find more information. This is awesome!" I replied.

"You know you can't take it home with you," Jessica teased.

"Nope, but I will be a proud adoptive parent and hang his or her photo on my wall," I said with a smirky grin.

My mind was set. I was going to adopt a manatee this year! As soon as I had this revelation, I remembered this magazine was printed in 2016 and then my mind wandered.

As Mr. Jones walked into the kitchen, he asked, "Why don't you go canoeing or kayaking at Blue Springs? You might see a bunch of manatees on a cool day like today."

My eyes widened as I looked at Jessica, wondering what she would say.

"How can I say anything *but* yes when my best friend is looking at me with puppy-dog eyes?" Jessica laughed.

"I will make your reservations and have them hold a kayak for you. You'll have fun!" Mr. Jones said as he made his way to the den.

The Jessica I knew would much rather go to a theme park than a state park. She liked animals, but they never trumped riding roller coasters or going shopping. It was not like her to want to check out nature, or manatees, all day. I didn't want to ask if she was sure about going in case she might change her mind. We would probably get in the car, start driving to Blue Springs State Park, and she would take a wrong exit and we would end up in the Universal parking lot. Now that was something I would halfway expect from her, but she seemed so convincing. Plus, she was letting Mr. Jones make a reservation and that didn't leave room for an exit plan. She liked Mr. Jones and wouldn't deceive him, nor have him go through the trouble of making reservations and then bail on them. It was almost as if she'd gone through a strange, groundbreaking personality change when arriving in Florida. Maybe she had fallen in love with Mother Nature.

Whatever the reason, I am going to get changed

for the adventure quickly before she changes her mind.

In a flash I was dressed for a new day of adventures with manatees. I met Jessica at the door, and we headed toward her car. Her phone connected to the car as she lowered the convertible top down, and she selected our destination on Maps, switched over to Spotify, and selected "Cheers," Jukebox the Ghost's newest album, and we sang out the first line. I wasn't thinking of all the neighbors who could hear us as we raised our glasses to more of the everyday, and for me, it was me who was dreaming and raising my glass to the victories of believing.

Before we knew it, we were taking the exit toward the park and following the signs to the parking area. The tall cypress trees led the way to a planked boardwalk that wound through the grove of hundred-foot-tall cypress trees. As we walked, critters jumped and scattered from the approaching strangers. A sign that read, "Please take nothing but pictures, leave nothing but footprints," hung near a sitting bench. An older couple sat huddled together, staying warm on this chilly day, as they poured over a state park map. Another couple stopped to take selfies in front of the largest cypress tree trunk, its base over twenty feet wide. They didn't look up or acknowledge us as we passed by, their attention captured with nature showing off its beauty all around us. The closer we got to the springs, the larger the cypress trees, and then the space opened and we found ourselves overlooking Blue Springs Run. The area looked like a cove sitting off the side of a slow-moving river, and the crystal-clear spring water revealed huge cypress tree roots, turtles peering up and catching their breath, and on the far side, dozens of gray blobs submerged, floating, resting, drawing close to one another—manatees. There were so many sea cows with their calves and possibly their yearlings as well. Several shapes and sizes gathered, and when more came into the area, they welcomed the new arrivals with open arms, or flippers. They were there for one another with a purpose, to stay warm and survive.

As we walked along the path toward the kayaking tours, we watched kids playing on the playground as their parents attempted to light a grill. Another couple we saw were pointing up, which caused everyone who saw to follow their fingers upward. They'd spotted a beautiful bald eagle gliding, seemingly floating, through the air above us. When I'd visualized Florida in my head prior to this spring break, I'd only pictured theme parks and massive crowds, but there was so much more.

It's a beautiful place.

Dear Journal,

As we kayaked down the St. Johns River, there were alligators warming in the sun, turtles by the dozens on top of logs, and cypress roots, and herons, limpkins, and several other types of birds on the shoreline and in the sky above. It was fun yet relaxing, and most important, Jess seemed to really enjoy herself. We absorbed all the sounds of nature, including critters conversing among themselves and scampering off, leaving their footprints as they scattered about. We laughed at a squirrel that looked as if he was tossing cypress nuts down for later, but then we realized he was trying to hit the people passing under him. At least that's what it looked like.

I will never forget this day, and it made me want to explore more, to be brave and go on adventures. There are so many places I haven't seen and critters I have not yet studied!

Feeling: Mother Nature enriched the Rose.

CHAPTER 9

STAR GAZING

Friday, 2nd of April

THE ONLY LIGHT THAT SNEAKED into the room danced off the glass ships "passing in the night" where the glimmering shine skipped up and onto a hand-carved anchor on a shelf. The decorative royal-blue anchor still hid in the darkness away from the ledge, but I could see the white painted letters that read, "Set your course by the stars, not by the lights of every passing ship. By Omar N. Bradley."

Adjusting my head, I forced it deeper into the cloud-like pillow and slowly turned onto my side. I felt empty, a little lost. I wasn't gloomy, but nor was I feeling happy. My eyes drifted up the wall, and I found myself whispering, "Dream catcher, I love my dreams because I am totally present for them, and I turn to them for guidance. Dreams answer my questions with greater understanding than I possess while awake. Although lately, I've had either no dreams or wacky dreams, and the thought of a lingering dream came back into focus. It was him again. Can I ask you to allow the good dreams in and catch the crazy ones?" Pulling the soft covers up, I rolled to my side and closed my eyes.

Oh, how I wish that request can be granted!

The room was brighter when I next woke up. Faintly I remembered myself floating in the air with Jessica. It was like a game or jumping on a trampoline, but we didn't bounce. We were laughing and having so much fun floating close to one another, dancing around, twirling, but then she turned and started to drift away. She was smiling and still dancing, she spun and laughed, but she was falling farther away from me and for some reason, I couldn't go with her. A warm feeling washed over me and then I opened my eyes, and the pillow's arched shape wrapped me in somewhat of a hug.

Dream catcher, you let another strange dream in!

My stomach lurched, and I had a sinking feeling that maybe Jessica was thinking of transferring to a university in Florida. I could tell she absolutely loved it here. She was in her element, so content, so peaceful and calm. Well, maybe she would wait to transfer schools if that was what she thought of doing. At least I hoped she would wait. We could move down to Florida together after graduation. It was only a year away, if we kept taking the extra class load. I shook the thoughts from my head—worrying about something that wasn't a thing was a waste of energy. It was time to get moving, so I pulled myself away from my soft pillow and began my morning tango with my hair. I couldn't wait to see what Jessica was up to today. I heard clanking and laughing coming from the kitchen and wondered if it was her or the mystery guest. I hurried to find out.

If I knew his name, I wouldn't have to call him the mystery man. It bothers me that I don't have the guts to ask.

Maybe the mystery man was with Jessica? Maybe after seeing her, he wouldn't even look at me. If I had told Jessica how I felt about him from the start, maybe she would know not to go out with him. My stomach lurched once more, and my fingers ran quickly back and forth over my necklace. When I arrived at the bottom of the staircase, I paused. A tingling sensation again ran up the back of my neck. Someone was nearby, in the music room. I didn't know if my feet would move. They felt frozen, and I wondered if they would be able to carry me anywhere. This house was neatly built to flow around in an open way. You could avoid a room, or someone in the room, by going in the opposite direction and still make it to your destination.

Maybe I will go the other direction.

Without another thought, I turned into the music room because curiosity had gotten the best of me, and a little nudge of bravery had surfaced too. I stopped when I saw it was Mrs. Jones. Using the lightest of steps, I walked slowly, hoping she wouldn't look up from what I assumed was a music book, because she was sitting on the small, cushioned seat at the grand piano as if she was going to play something. I somehow missed all the creaks in the floor, which was an accomplishment, thankful not to have caught her attention.

At least today she isn't staring off at nowhere or crying.

Maybe it's a good day and we can finally, officially meet her, but I still didn't want to bother her while she was most likely in her "leave-me-alone" time for reflection and meditation.

The sound of a piano key being pressed echoed through the house, and the kitchen noise silenced. A cord was heard, then a few more notes and she stopped. I heard whispering coming from the kitchen and took another step but fell still once more when the music began again. I then hurried my steps into the kitchen, hoping she wouldn't stop because of me.

Standing near Jessica, Mr. Jones whispered, "The song is 'And We Will Shine,' by Dirk Maassen. He's a pianist originally from the Netherlands. My wife learned to play this song by ear. She will look and look through her piano books but seems to always revert to playing his song. It's great to hear her play again. I think she is working out her feelings, and that is a good sign. She was the best thing that ever happened to me, and I can't stand to see her sad."

We stood over the warm pancakes Mr. Jones had just flipped off the skillet, onto the serving plate. It was tranquil, and I could feel the piano music soaking into my body.

"She is an amazing piano player!" I said after the song was complete and before she started again.

"Oh, good, she's playing another song." Mr. Jones smiled, and his gaze seemed to linger toward where his wife was in the music room as his body swayed slightly with the song. He glanced down at the floor before turning back toward us and asked, "Do you recognize this song?" His deep thoughtful eyes and the tone of his voice were filled with love as he thought of the name of the song himself.

Jessica and I looked at one another, listened for another measure or two as I ran my necklace between my fingers for a slight moment, and then we grinned as we both remembered at the same time. She hesitated before answering because we were not sure it was a question he needed us to answer.

"Is it 'Someone You Loved' by Lewis Capaldi?" Jessica replied softly, only knowing the song because she'd sung it in choir during her senior year of high school.

He responded with a longing look. "I used to play the viola along with her, when I could play." His gaze found the skillet, and he reached for the knob and turned the burner off. "Enjoy your pancakes, you two." His ginned faded before he turned and drifted out of the kitchen.

I hoped he was going to join his wife and play something with her but caught the "when I could play" and his glance down toward the floor. I wondered if playing viola was hard on aging hands.

We ate in silence and then cleaned and put the dishes away quietly as we listened to Mrs. Jones pour over the piano like a long-lost friend. As I followed Jessica out the back door toward the pool area, I saw Mrs. Jones playing and, for a brief second, thought I saw Mr. Jones's shadow. He was holding his viola as if to play, but when the door shut, I could no longer hear the music or see them and knew it would be rude to stare.

Later, Mr. Jones joined us outside in the shaded sitting area, where he started to prune and check the soil in the garden. In his usual way, he explained what he was doing and talked about the types of plants in that garden and their purpose in life.

"These are Hoya carnosa plants. See the pink-and-red star-shaped flowers that seem as delicate as porcelain, budding among deep-green waxy vines?" Mr. Jones said.

"They almost look fake," Jessica said as we watched Mr. Jones tenderly pull and weave the new growth around the trellis.

"These are also called star flowers. They seem

to love the humidity and shade out here," Mr. Jones said as he concentrated on his task. "Speaking of stars, I will set the telescope out in the backyard for you two to stargaze tonight."

We thanked him, and he disappeared into the house.

Jessica challenged me to the world's largest putting pool-table game. It was a combination of billiards and mini golf. We rolled the game's green felt surface out and attached the edges, including the six pool pockets, and found the instructions. We gathered the golf balls, which were painted to resemble billiard balls, and placed all except the white cue ball into the triangle ball rack as directed in the instructions. We chose our golf putters and took turns dropping the cue ball down. The drop closest to a pocket without falling in got to break. We played 8-ball and switched to 9-ball as the sun drifted from late morning to the afternoon. When Jessica accidentally hit her ball off the pad and it bounced into the real pool, we looked at one another.

"I'll get it," I said.

She quickly responded, "No, no, no, I'll get my ball!" She grabbed my arm to hold me back, and we danced around one another, trying to get to the pool first until we reached the edge of the pool and both dove in, laughing. Coming up for air, we spun around looking for the ball, and the race to the ball began. In and out of the pool was where we stayed until evening.

After dark, we made our way out to the fire pit area where Mr. Jones stood looking through the huge telescope. I would have believed he borrowed it from NASA if that's what he told me, because his stories were so incredible, and I could only dream of living a life as full as his had been.

"If there were no night, we would not realize the importance of day, nor could we see the stars and the massiveness of the universe out in the stars we live," Mr. Jones proclaimed.

"That was beautiful, and so true!" replied Jessica.

The moon was hiding, and the city lights were dim, being miles away, allowing twinkling stars and planets above us to seem extra bright. It was strange to think some of those stars were millions of light-years away when they looked close enough to touch.

"Look, a shooting star!" Jessica shrieked with excitement as she pointed.

"Do you think we'll see any meteor showers?" I asked Mr. Jones.

"It is an endless wonder in the sky above," he replied with a laugh. "Even the ancient cultures built structures like the pyramids in Egypt and Machu Picchu in Peru to align with the phases of the moon, the sun, and the solstices."

"How does the saying go, look up at the stars and not down at your feet," stated Jessica.

"Who could look down on a night like tonight?" I replied. "I used to sleep on the deck of our boat on nights like these, but we didn't have a telescope."

Mr. Jones smiled at us and said, "So, girls, gaze up to the heavens, know we are a mere speck in the universe, and let yourself experience the depth of existence. Enjoy! I will bring the telescope inside when you are done stargazing."

Mr. Jones left so quickly that I didn't see him leave, but my head was up with the stars.

Dear Journal,

While gazing up to the sky and watching the twinkling light show tonight, I felt the world rotating. It felt like it was spinning out of control and there was nothing I could do to slow it. It was painful knowing I was so helpless. I realized what a mere tiny speck in the universe I really am.

Thinking of Mrs. Jones playing the piano reminded me of how much music, the tempo, can help calm a person. Maybe being back at the piano will help her. I know when riding a horse, my heart feels rhythmically together with theirs, but while not being able to ride and feel that connection…my tempo seems off.

Maybe I should start playing an instrument. There are so many things I should do in my life, it is hard to know which one to start with.

As humans, we must take the bad with the good and appreciate everything, because we are not in control of *anything* like we might think we are. My gaze was drawn back to one star again and again. I watched it sparkle and felt, I guess, an unexpected connection. As if I were a child again, I tried to make a wish on that star but didn't know if I should make the wish for myself or for others. Is it selfish to wish for your own bravery, health, or even love? Like a child, I found that star to be a friend and knew it could grant a wish in the most beautiful way, but only if I could find my deepest desire, the wish I would want the most.

Star light, star bright, the most beautiful star I saw tonight, I wish I may, I wish I might have the wish I say tonight…

Let the pain cease to exist, surrender control, and sing out to the stars.

Feeling: Humbled by knowing we are a mere speck in the universe, but I am no longer an ethereal Rose.

CHAPTER 10

THE LIGHTHOUSE

Saturday, 3rd of April

Not a sound in the house could be heard as I drifted awake, nor was there a sparkle of sunshine trying to find me through the curtain hanging in front of the window. I felt as light as my pillow while rolling over to my other side, then I noticed something new.

How did I miss this?

An iconic, very famous painting by William Daniell was leaning against the wall, as if a storm had knocked it down. This was the famous *Eddystone Lighthouse, During a Storm* print. The original was painted around 1825, and from my bed it looked like it could be the original.

When we lived on the sailboat, Dad had only a few books on board and most of them were about lighthouses or lighthouse art. This one was one of my favorites, I guess because of the way it shows dramatic light contrast between the dark swelling seas as they engulf the lighthouse and the concentrating beam of light shining from the lantern room. I remember thinking of how I wouldn't want to be out sailing on those seas. Dad had once told me that lighthouse dreams usually meant you were seeking guidance. It could also be a symbol of hope, or a life landmark, or even danger. The beacon also reflected exalted feelings and trying to overcome obstacles.

Maybe it's me seeking out a way to speak to the man I dreamed of. He visited me again last night.

Something was drawing me to this piece of art, and it wasn't the weather or the sailing conditions. I ran my necklace between my fingers and thought about the lighthouse in the painting. It was located on the Eddystone Rocks near the village named Rame Head in England. The beam of light in the painting was the only illumination in the scene, glowing upon the dark, ravishing waves that were trying to snuff the beacon out. Now the painting was right in front of me, where I could see the brilliant yellow tones coming from the lantern room as if it were warning me of upcoming obstacles or danger ahead. Or was the lighthouse trying to give me hope and guide me, and if so, where? I found myself oddly asking the dream catcher. And why hadn't I noticed this striking piece of art before?

I closed my eyes, drifting back to sleep.

As I woke again a while later, I slowly remembered the painting, but when I turned over to look at it again, it wasn't there. The sea star dream catcher was broken in two pieces, which didn't make sense. The only thing left hanging on the wall was the weaving that oddly made it look like a doily. The only thing I could think of was that I must have thrashed around in my sleep, like the waves in the painting. Maybe I did this to the dream catcher, but why?

My arms felt the burden of my weight as I lifted myself up into a sitting position. The world spun a little too fast for me to get my bearings to stand, and the moment I placed my feet on the floor, the weight of emotions anchored my whole body to the floor. As if my feet were filled with concrete, I dragged myself off the bed, found a swimsuit and cover shirt, and slowly dragged myself down the stairs, where I saw Jessica floating in the pool. The urge to cry crossed my mind and slugged my gut. Maybe it's knowing, and dreading, that spring break was almost over. We would be leaving Florida soon and going back to school to finish the semester. This was weighing on me more than I realized.

I've been on the verge of crying a few times since I woke up. Why?!

I stepped outside and trod over to the pool, asking Jessica, "Where did you find that pool float? It looks as if you're a cherub." I heard my own voice crack. It sounded as tired as my body felt.

"What, this little thing?" she said as she waved

her hands over the wings off to the side of her head-rest. "Isn't it great! It is one of the most comfortable things ever, and it's as if I am floating."

"You are floating, Jess!" I said, and then we broke out into laughter. "Oh, I want one. Maybe I will feel better floating too!" I teased.

"Nope, there is only one, and I have dibs. Well, there is a plain float without the wings hidden in the pool house shower." Jessica laughed. "You're not an angel like me." She winked at me.

I gave her a look and batted my eyelids so she could see the emphasis of my words. "I could be if I wanted." Then I made my way into the pool house in search of a pool float of my own.

Our laughter made the air light, my feet not as heavy as I glided my way to the pool house in search of any kind of float. I found one much like hers but without the cherub wings and took it with me back to the pool.

"Mr. Jones said it's a fishing day, if you want to fish, that is. He said we are having fish tacos tonight and he's making homemade salsa, made from the garden!"

As Jessica spoke, I wondered if she wanted to fish or if she wanted to do something more exciting for our last day here. With my melancholy mood, I was fearful of sitting around too much, but accord-ing to Florida Fish and Wildlife, the first Saturday in April was one of two license-free fishing days and our three-day pass had ended. Today was the last day we could see if we could catch a fish.

"Wait, do you want to fish for real?" Jessica asked.

"Only if you do," I replied, glancing at Jessica. I knew what she wanted to do the second she looked over at me.

"Why not! Let's do it!" Jessica practically cheered. "Let's catch the Joneses some fish!"

Several hours later, Jessica had caught nothing but fish, and several of them, all of legal length and weight. I, on the other hand, caught several things other than fish, including weeds, some trash, and a turtle. Jessica had to help with the turtle, but no worries, we got the hook off him and sent him on his merry way, probably to recuperate on a log somewhere far away from the dock. I really thought the turtle just wanted to come visit and didn't realize what a bad idea it would be until it was too late.

"It looks like you have a Florida superpower—fishing!" I said as Jessica reeled in her sixth fish of the day.

She smiled, holding up her biggest catch, and replied, "Looks like you have helped their local Keep Lake Beautiful organization by pulling some garbage out of Lake Minnehaha. Way to go volunteering today," she added with a wink.

Mr. Jones took our fish, and we sat inside the screened deck drinking sodas from the dorm-room-sized refrigerator while laughing and reminiscing about our days here.

"Do you think you can join one or more of my study groups? They are really nice people and smart like you are. I think you would like them, if you could give them a chance," Jessica said.

"Maybe I will!" I said with positive affirmation, then I noticed Jessica smile, and it brightened her whole face. I didn't feel the hesitation I had normally felt, and I was sure I could now try to join her study group.

"Jessica," I said softly, "thank you for bringing me here and for this experience."

Jessica nodded and smiled, then her gaze was pulled back out beyond the lake shoreline. "That's what best friends do!" she whispered softly.

After a while we made our way back toward the house, where Mr. Jones had started preparing fish tacos. He used herbs and vegetables from the garden and added some pineapple and mango bits to the salsa, which was delicious. He showed Jessica and me how to make homemade tortillas, and it was easier than I'd expected. We sat and ate under the pergola, where the lights made it look as if we were sitting in a little restaurant in Italy. I chose the seat next to Mr. Jones, and Jessica sat on my other side. We laughed and looked out onto the lake—this was lake life at its best!

"Dinner was outstanding again, Mr. Jones! Thank you," I said as I picked our dishes up off the table.

"You are very welcome!" He smiled and then asked, "How did you enjoy the *Girl Sailing* book? I thought you might like it because you grew up on a sailboat."

"I can relate to Annie mainly because of living on a sailboat. However, up until sixth grade, I had lived on a sailboat my *entire* life. Unlike Annie, who went through an array of emotions at the beginning because she was ripped away from life as she knew it on her horse farm in southern California. She journaled to cope. I journal…because…I find inspiration from each day lived in hopes for my future, that one day I will get to experience more by putting myself out there." Suddenly my face flushed, and I turned away from him and started gathering more dishes to take inside. *Why did I tell him why I journal?*

Mr. Jones replied, "The lesson from *Girl Sailing* was about more than Annie learning how to sail a boat, jet ski, chart out a course, scuba dive. It's about letting go, trusting the adventure your life has in store for you, and growing from all experiences, the good and the bad, that come your way."

I mused as I ran my necklace between my fingers, then turned back toward him and said, "You're right! Thank you for sharing that with me." I picked the remaining dishes up from the table and walked them into the house.

Dear Journal,

The room fell quiet with Jess much less talkative, and I didn't want to share what was on my mind. Jessica is the only person I can talk to, but there was never the right moment to bring up this guy I had never met and yet couldn't get off my mind. She seems to be lost in her own thoughts and probably dreading the drive back to school. Mr. Jones told me tomorrow is a new moon and a new moon represents new beginnings. Maybe Jessica is affected by the new moon. It is something to think about, anyway.

Tonight, I have little hope of meeting the man who makes my heart skip a beat. Our time is coming to an end, and reality will be flashing before us as we head home tomorrow. My ears are listening for the door chime. If I stay awake a little longer, maybe he will come in and I can make an excuse to meet him in the kitchen or even at the front door.

Feeling: Rose has her feet planted firmly in the soil, but her petals are blowing off in the wind.

CHAPTER 11

ROSE'S NIGHTMARE

BEEP, BEEP, BEEP.

I rolled over to get farther away from the noise, but the pain was unbearable.

Beep, beep, beep.

I tried to grab the second pillow on the bed and sandwich my head with them both in hopes of drowning out the constant sound of Mr. Jones's alarm, but then the smell of stale coffee wafted in and lingered. My mind started to drift as I woke, and an unusual scent engulfed my nose.

No single-serve fresh coffee I've ever had smells like this!

This was the smell of day-old coffee, burned coffee left in the dorm's lounge overnight. I opened my eyes, almost dreaming I was somewhere else, not my bed at the B&B. Confused, I closed my eyes and slowly opened them again, and the nautical room finally took shape. The only thing I smelled was citrus and bleach.

What is going on downstairs?

Jessica could have been making orange juice again, or maybe Mr. Jones was cleaning something with one of his citrus concoctions, but why could I smell it in my room? I closed my eyes and drifted away.

What does it mean to smell things in dreams?

My body was light, floating. I was scuba diving in the ocean. Or maybe free diving like Jessica was the other day, but unlike Jess, I needed air and started to panic. Unknown obstacles stood in the way of my rising to the surface. Gasping for air, my arms flailed. I was caught in kelp or a fishnet, and then it started to sting and I couldn't see what it was. A loud *beep, beep, beep* pulsed in my ears, gradually growing even louder. Something was under the water with me, and this thought made my heart race. It was chasing me! I continued to swim, fighting like hell from what was tugging at my wrists, and growing more desperate for air. Teeth dug into my arm like needles piercing my skin. My arm was useless, constrained, and I felt warm liquid flowing over my skin. Was I bleeding? Through the water, I heard cheers, several people, a crowd. Was I in a competition, a race? The people sounded close, but…

How could this be? I am underwater!

"Fight, Rose! Fight! Come on, Rose. Come back to us."

The voices seemed to be coming from people I knew, but I wasn't sure. A faint beeping sound pulsed over the din of several hurried footsteps echoing off in the distance.

Am I awake?

Beep, beep, beep sounds intertwined with *clank, clunk, ping* sounds.

I turned over to my side and grabbed the dream catcher, gasping for breath. My chest heaved, and my mouth was dry. My head felt light, yet foggy.

It's official. That was the strangest dream ever, but I can breathe!

My body ached as if I had been sleeping on a mattress filled with pebbles from the beach. I tugged at my new favorite pillow, but it was hard, flat, and the pillow cover felt rough, scratchy to touch. The buzzing and continuous *beep, beep, beep* was no longer off in the distance but sounded like it was coming from the glass fishing-float light that hung near my bed.

Drugged, I am drugged, like the feeling I had the day Jess and I arrived here.

The fog engulfed me. My eyes were not able to focus. My fisherman's float light looked square, like something sitting on a pole instead of hanging from the ceiling. I felt tired and needed to close my eyes. I let myself drift in and out of sleep, but I couldn't understand the pain. Everything went dark. I was falling back to sleep but didn't want to dream again. When I could, I slowly opened my eyes, squinting at bright lights shining down on me and cold air raising every hair on my arms upward.

"Who turned on the lights?" I said as I looked up at the strange florescent lights above my bed.

"Rose. Rose. Are you there? Wake up!" My mother's voice came soft, unclear, from somewhere in the room.

I reached for my phone, thinking I must have fallen asleep while talking on the phone. But my phone fell in the water and no longer worked. Maybe she called Jessica, and it was Jessica's phone. I said "Hello" without seeing the phone.

"I'm here, but why are *you* here?" I said before realizing no sound was coming out of my mouth. I opened my eyes and tried to move, even sit, but a shock of pain ran through my body like a lightning bolt.

Wait, where am I?

I heard myself moan under the enormous amount of pain ripping through my body.

What the heck?! Who is in my room? Why are they hurting me?

"It's all right, baby. We are here," my parents' voices rang out.

What are Mom and Dad doing in Florida?

I forced my eyes back open through the pain and

wondered where I could be. "Mom! Dad?" I said, my voice scratchy like a whisper because my throat was dry as the desert.

I believe I swallowed a cactus.

My watery eyes felt dry and burned and wouldn't focus. My gaze slowly drifted around the bright, fuzzy, white room. There were monitors on the side of my bed with cords attached to my chest. My arm was wrapped with thick bandages, cast-like. Two IV bags hung from a pole nearby, attached to tubes taped to needles that protruded from my wrists, which were lightly covered with fresh blood. Doctors and nurses scurried around my bed, shined bright lights in my eyes, and took several notes on their handheld computer pads. I wanted my mom, but someone led her away and put her in a chair across the room. These people came by the droves, walking in and out the door. Whispers and hurried footsteps. I faded in and out, and whenever I opened my eyes, someone new was hovering over me.

My hair is probably a mess. I should put it up before I go downstairs and see Jess. I drifted back to sleep.

When I opened my eyes again, I was so confused. Studying the room through the blurry fog, I started piecing everything together. My gaze rounded the small room, stopping at the white roses and gardenias in a vase the shape of a wave sitting on a shelf. A familiar-looking book was laying on the tray between my bed and where my mother sat. She stood and stepped closer to my bed and reached out for the book that my eyes seemed to be studying. She said, "I've been reading *Girl Sailing Aboard the Western Star* to you every day while you were, well, sleeping." She told me a summary of the book, which sounded like something I would read.

"Sorry, I don't remember you reading," I hoarsely whispered.

Conversations weren't long, as I drifted in and out, but every time I woke up, it seemed more peaceful, with fewer people running in and out. I was more confused each time, though, baffled because my memories were askew.

Mom's eyes were a fire red, swollen and filled with tears, when she felt brave enough to speak again. "I prayed you wouldn't follow the light with Jessica." She looked down at my hands and placed her frail, soft hand on mine, tears streaming down her cheeks.

Follow Jessica?

Together, Mom and Dad told me about a car accident. As they spoke, I could feel tears flowing from my eyes, but the story didn't seem real. If it was, who was it about? Who had an accident? Everything was unclear, because what they were telling me was not what I remembered.

Jessica and I were at the Lakehouse. We were so happy! So happy it was as if we were floating on air!

Slowly, Dad put his hand on mine and softly said, "Jessica didn't make it."

"Jess didn't make it *where*?" I asked. Confused, my gaze drifted from Mom to Dad and back again.

A wave of sadness washed over me, and the ocean current started to pull me under again, I could hardly catch my breath. *Jess was just with me last night. We watched the Disney fireworks again while sitting by the firepit.* I struggled for clarity. A glimpse of Jessica floating. A recollection. We were floating together. A warm feeling flushed over me. In my memories, she was extremely happy and full of love. I recalled her swimming underwater for too long. It had felt like minutes before she broke the surface for air, and even then, she wasn't winded. She wasn't herself either. She spoke of being free, floating on clouds, and angels.

Another memory flashed into my head. Jessica yelled into the wind on the bow of the Hobie Wave, "I'm light as a feather and free as a cloud." I could see her arms stretched out, ready to fly.

A vision of us spinning and swirling together in a dust storm with car parts mixed and thrashing about around us. *We were flying.*

Oh no!

Jessica started floating farther away from me, and I couldn't reach her.

I didn't go with her.

I remembered her voice, her blue eyes staring into mine as clear as ever, and she said, "Rose, promise me you will not be sad." I'd seen her as an angel in the pool and asked her for a float like hers, and she'd said I wasn't an angel.

We never made it to the lake house. My mind raced. *That can't be true.*

"Mom, I promise, we were at the B&B. On spring break," I argued. "It's in my journal. Find my journal."

Mom went over to the only closet in the hospital room and opened it, exposing my oversized carry bag. It looked old, worn, dirty, and very tattered. She dug in the bag until she found my journal and then showed me the last entry from Tuesday, the twenty-third of March. The day at school when I was feeling so overwhelmed with other people's feelings and emotions.

"That's not my bag! It's not my journal! Where are my things?" I yelled.

"I am so sorry, honey." She paused before saying, "Jessica didn't make it after the car accident. She died."

"You were on the way to your Florida vacation," my dad said in a caring tone that felt as if it rang out harshly. All I heard were words that seemed to scream out to me, that fell on me like a spinning car.

When I tried to force myself to sit up, my arm jerked and I grimaced with pain, but I pulled myself to the edge of the hospital bed anyway. There I paused, only because my head felt light. I was going to puke. *Is the room spinning?*

"This can't be real," I sobbed out.

I leaned forward and the earth rotated. I reached out and held onto the only thing that seemed still but couldn't stop myself from falling. I twisted, moving myself off the bed, knowing if I fell it would hurt, but I needed to stand. I needed to go find Jessica!

My legs failed me, but someone's arms caught me before I hit the floor.

A man, his chest as blue as the sky and his voice deep, softly said, "Hold up, you're not ready to stand up quite yet."

The hairs on the back of my neck twitched because his voice was oddly familiar. But why?

He must be my doctor?

It felt like fog drifted in and settled over my brain again. The man's solid frame, his soft blue scrubs, his strong arms holding me, strangely comforted me. A tickling sensation ran around my neck, my face reddened, and even my ears felt warm. I attempted to push him away, but his hands only allowed me to lean far enough away for our eyes to meet. His deep-brown eyes met mine, and a tingling sensation ran underneath my hair, around my neck, causing goosebumps to flush over my face and even my ears. I wanted to place my hand behind my neck, but I couldn't and didn't want to let go. My whole body quivered and then surged forward, crashing into his tall, lean frame. How embarrassing to meet the mystery guest by tripping and falling into his arms.

Then I realized I was not at the lake house, and

he was my doctor. My stomach turned and my head spun. I pressed my head into his chest and wrapped my arms around him as rivers streamed from my eyes. He waited patiently and then gently placed me back onto the bed as I reached up to rub my necklace, but it wasn't there. The last thing I wanted to do was let go of the only thing that seemed familiar at that moment—this stranger holding me in his arms.

Mom watched me closely, knowing the only thing that comforted me when I was nervous was rubbing my gold ship chain necklace. The necklace Dad and I found when we dove an old shipwreck near the Dominican Republic. The doctor stepped away as my mother came closer.

"Rose, your necklace is right here." Mom held her hand out. "They had to take it off you when you arrived. Where did you get the beautiful gold conch shell pendant?" She held the pendant closer for me to see.

I remember Jessica handing me a conch shell while floating in water, I think.

A tear ran down my cheek, and as if Mom knew what to do for me at that moment, she secured my necklace back around my neck and didn't wait for a reply. I ran my fingers over the chain, as I had for so many years, but this time I stopped at the conch shell pendant. I studied the shape and every groove with the tips of my fingers, then closed my eyes and tried to remember, tried to sort the dream away from this nightmare.

CHAPTER 12

THE LAKEHOUSE RETREAT

Tuesday, 29th day of March

MY LIFE CHANGED A YEAR ago this week. The sun bounced off my red Jeep Wrangler, practically blinding me as I pulled into the driveway of the two-story B&B lake house. My fingers gripped the steering wheel firmly as I sat looking toward the front door. My heart raced, and my mind seemed to be stuck in a fog. The sounds made by a seven-foot-tall classic antique cherub-angel three-tiered water fountain faintly spoke to me with the sounds of water dripping, splashing, and bubbling. I pulled my gaze from the house, tapped my passcode into my phone, and opened the B&B app to the confirmation page.

Jessica would be proud of me, traveling all by myself, and I didn't kill a tree. I am trusting the app on my new phone!

Mrs. Jones introduced herself to me at the front

door and led me inside, where a breathtaking large, framed image of a lighthouse hung just inside the entryway. It was a photograph taken on a picture-perfect day, the sky clear and blue with specks of birds in flight. A white, sandy beach stretched out, leading the way to a lighthouse built in the mid to late 1800s. Its tapered brick cylindrical tower was painted white and the balcony and lantern room black. Black coral protruded from the water to the base, as a couple of palm trees swayed nearby. It's the kind of picture you look at and feel the need to take a deep breath, relaxing and beautiful. Along the bottom of the frame was a plaque that read: "You are my lighthouse that brings me home, no matter how dark the seas."

"My husband took that photo and wrote that quote. He had it framed for our anniversary." Her expression showed the importance of this image. Her eyes left mine to gaze up at it. "I didn't know about this picture for almost a year after his passing. He had only given the framers his cell phone number, hoping to keep it a surprise for me."

My heart felt a deep emptiness inside. I sensed the void, the hole in her heart left by her husband's passing. I stood quietly, knowing she had more to say and couldn't find the words. My gaze landed on the small, framed photograph of the two of them standing on the dock with a large house behind them, the photograph I'd seen on the website with Jessica. Mr.

Jones was a kind-looking man, I thought. My attention was back to Mrs. Jones as she looked into my eyes and said, "He passed away a few days before our anniversary last year." She looked down at her hands and caressed her wedding ring. "It was March twenty-sixth, and our anniversary is April second, sixty-five years ago." She reached out and took my hand, and together for a moment, my mind and body engulfed her deep sorrow. However, as she held my hand firmly, I battled with the date of his passing.

The day before Jessica and I had the accident.

Mrs. Jones looked exactly as I remembered from the picture on the B&B website, the one Jessica and I had visited so many times prior to booking our rooms. She didn't know about our accident. We hadn't received the notice of cancellation she'd sent out when her husband passed, because we never checked our emails that day. Then it was too late. We had the accident and obviously didn't show up for our reservations. In case Mrs. Jones asked about Jessica, or my friend who was supposed to come with me last year, I had decided to keep the accident to myself, or at least the date of the accident. I didn't need to burden her with something that happened a year ago and didn't concern her. Even if we'd gotten the message, we would have gone to Florida. We might have stayed somewhere on the beach or a theme park, but we would have driven down here no matter what.

Trust your instincts and your intuition, Rose!

A sudden surge of chill bumps ran all over my body. Jessica's laugh, Mr. Jones's slight smile—I could hear and see them as plain as the scars on my arm. An intense feeling of peace and happiness blanketed me, releasing the deep feeling of sorrow.

Mrs. Jones gave me a quick tour of the house and guided me outside to show me the unique gardens she and her husband had created.

"This is an amazing garden you have here, and you do all the work?" I asked Mrs. Jones.

Mrs. Jones wrapped both of her arms around herself, almost in a hug. "I don't feel like I am taking care of the garden alone. Sometimes I feel him here with me, even helping me," she said as she carried on. "He would always tell our guests about how they shouldn't be bothered by mosquitoes because we planted an assortment of plants that are nature's way of shooing those pesky things away." She smiled and turned toward the planters, gardens, and then large pots. "We are growing oregano, basil, and several other multipurpose plants."

A hint of fresh spaghetti sauce was in our future, I hoped, since it was my favorite food.

She walked and spoke as if remembering word for word what her husband once told the guests or friends visiting. "Lemongrass lines the sidewalks in front of the dwarf citrus trees growing in large pots. Thyme is planted in the critter-shaped pots near the sitting areas and bloom the sweetest little flowers. The rosemary plants are pruned into topiary shapes. My favorites are the ones shaped into hearts." She spoke softly, caringly, then smiled and stopped next to one of the heart-shaped rosemary plants and tugged at the small branches, tucking them around, trying to train the new growth into the heart shape.

As I watched her, I took in the fragrances and the sounds around us. Everything was so peaceful here, and I didn't realize how much I enjoy rosemary fragrance until now.

Our next stop was the pineapple plants. She bent over to smell them, felt their firmness, and picked the ripest pineapple. She sniffed the bottom again and gave it to me to touch and smell. "A ripe pineapple should have a firm shell but not too hard. You know it's ripe when you squeeze. It should give in, and the bottom should smell distinctively like a sweet pine-apple. Once you pick a pineapple, they stop growing and sweetening. It's true you can leave it out or bag it and it will become softer and juicier, but they will not get any sweeter from the time they are chosen," she said.

I sniffed in the sweet smell.

She smiled and said, "This one Mr. Jones would have been proud of!"

I followed her into the kitchen, and she handed me the large knife. I attempted to cut it, trying my best to make it look nice. I wasn't sure where I'd learned how to cut a pineapple, but this one ended up looking like a piece of art. I shocked myself, and by the looks of Mrs. Jones, I shocked her as well.

My brain must have soaked up more from Pinterest than I thought.

Spending time with Mrs. Jones was like spending time with family rather than a B&B host. It was like visiting the nicest grandmother in the world. No offense to my own grandmothers, who I loved dearly.

"Rose, would you like to help me make pasta sauce? I have some tomatoes already prepped, peeled, and starting to simmer. They need stirring and seasoning," Mrs. Jones said.

I nodded and grinned, replying, "Mrs. Jones, I was hoping you would ask!"

"Oh, please, call me Kathie," she said with a smile and then pointed up toward the built-in pantry. "The spices are in this cupboard." She opened it and laid the recipe on the counter for me to follow.

"Are all of these spices from your garden?" I asked as I looked through the different mixtures of dried basil, oregano, red pepper mixes, rosemary, thyme, and several more. "Is this considered garden-to-table eating?"

"Yes, it is! I cut and dry all the seasonings, and these are the easiest vegetables to grow in a garden. For dinner tonight, the only thing we must use store-bought is flour and eggs. I would have my own eggs, but the neighbors would complain about the chickens." She giggled, probably at the thought of having chickens in this neighborhood.

"What are flour and eggs used for?" I asked.

"Oh, we make our own pasta!" She smiled at me and pointed to a pasta-making machine.

Looking in the direction she was pointing, I saw the machine and said, "That's right!" I grinned but was puzzled as to why I'd said that as if I had made homemade pasta before. Then I turned my attention back to the sauce and started adding the seasonings and stirring the pot slowly. I cupped my hand and waved the scent over to my nose and sniffed. Something was missing, so I dug around in a drawer and found a store-bought seasoning container, but the label was torn off. I took a long look at the reddish-colored ingredients, opened it, and gave a little smell.

Perfect!

I added the "secret spice," with a dash here and there, took the long wooden spoon and stirred the new spice into the sauce, and then waved another smell over to my nose. I noticed Mrs. Jones watching me add the spice that was not on her list and felt my face flush. Out of my mouth spilled, "Spice a dish with love and it pleases every palate!"

Mrs. Jones's shocked expression surprised me. She stood still, her face pale as she wobbled and then her legs buckled. In a flash, the young man now living in the downstairs bedroom walked into the kitchen, saw Mrs. Jones weaken, and caught her before she fell. He lowered her into a chair and found her pulse. His gaze met mine, and we held it too long, but I couldn't turn away, nor could he. He had the deepest dark-brown eyes I had ever seen.

Breaking the silence he said, "You know, eyes are the window to the soul."

I blushed, blinked, and smiled before I turned toward the kitchen to get Mrs. Jones a glass of water.

Mrs. Jones's face color changed to a rosy pink, and she muttered, "Where are my manners? I haven't introduced the both of you. Rose, this is Jes. He has been staying with us, I mean at our—*my*—B&B for years. Now he is my permanent renter." She looked down at the floor, trying to regain her composure over the mixed feeling of now being the sole owner of the house. "Jes came to the Orlando area for work and a little bit of leisure and now works in Orlando full time." She smiled, returning to her normal self, and reached for our hands and placed them together as if we had forgotten how to move our bodies and shake hands in greeting.

My face reddened, and Jes grinned. His whole body shivered, and he suddenly tried to explain his unanticipated body movement. "I must have gotten a little chill from the air conditioner."

But I hadn't heard the air conditioner run.

"I am on vacation this week from work, because on the last Tuesday of the month, I go over to Anna Marie Island and do sand sculptures on the beach with my old buddies from college. It's tomorrow. Go with me. It will be fun," Jes said as if we had known one another for years.

I replied with an unexpected and swift, "Sure, that sounds fun."

Then we both noticed our hands had remained together in a shakeless grip. We slowly released our grips, as if not wanting to relinquish the warmth of our touch.

It took a minute to compose myself and take charge of my thoughts. I walked back into the kitchen to stir the sauce one more time before replacing the lid.

Feeling the need to catch my breath I decided to wander through the house and take a closer look at all the great art the Joneses had collected throughout the years. As I started to leave the kitchen area, I asked Jes, "Have we met before?" His tall athletic frame and all-American look, maybe just a familiar face, made me feel as if I had seen him before. Maybe he was in the Olympics or played baseball?

He hesitated before replying, "I don't think so."

To clear my thoughts, I started meandering around the house. The photographs of this house on the B&B website made me feel like I was here before, probably because Jessica and I spent hours researching and looking at the pictures. As I casually walked around the living room, admiring the photographs and artwork, I noticed a hand-blown glass vase in the shape of a wave.

Where have I seen that before?

The vase sat near a Wyland bronze whale tail sculpture just like the one I saw in the Wyland art gallery a few months ago. I have always been a fan of Wyland, but this bronze had made the hairs on the back of my neck stand straight up. It was such a strong déjà vu moment, one I could never forget. In this moment, I wondered if the thought of the gallery gave me the same feeling. I inhaled and exhaled slowly while observing the bronze's beauty, then I continued wandering. I stopped at a photograph of a gigantic manatee sand sculpture. The details were extraordinary. Somehow the sculptor had captured the manatee in motion as she and her calf ate seagrass.

A tickling sensation ran around my neck, my face reddened, and even my ears felt warm. I rotated my head slowly around in a circular motion, placed my hands behind my neck, and lifted my thick brown curls, hoping this would cool me. I couldn't control the urge, and my whole body quivered. My heart pulsed in my ears, and I felt it skip a beat inside my chest. My knees buckled slightly, so I placed my hand on the small table to steady myself where I noticed a beautiful conch shell sitting on top of what looked to be a piece of a dream catcher. My shaking fingers instantly found my necklace and slid down the ship chain until I felt the conch shell pendant and caressed it.

I picked the real shell up off the table and held it to my ear, hoping the sound of the sea from within would settle my sporadic heartbeat. With my eyes closed tightly, I held the cool shell against my cheek, and with my free hand, my fingers glided over my ship chain necklace. The sound of the ocean gently soothed me, the same way Jessica's laugh had always had a magical way of calming me. I opened my eyes, my gaze landing on the photograph of the sand sculpture. A sense of strength and warmth washed over me like a ray of sunshine falling onto my skin.

This seems so familiar…déjà vu.

Gently, I placed the shell back on the dream catcher doily as a soft tingling sensation ran through my body. But this time it was a feeling of home, amity, and comfort.

"Manatees are one of my favorite things in the world," Jes whispered as he appeared from nowhere, now standing right behind me.

I turned to face him, feeling the warmth of his deep-brown eyes as he gazed into mine. The sparkle of the gold flakes brightened the brown color of his eyes, somehow drawing me in closer. I found some words to mutter out, "I adopted a manatee named Charles from Save the Manatee organization a few months ago."

Jes smiled and nodded, then asked, "Can I join you on this little walking art tour?"

My only response was a nod, because I couldn't shake how familiar he was to me. I meandered through the room, Jes following close behind.

"Have you been to Florida before?" Jes curiously asked.

"One year ago, I was heading this way." I glanced down at the scar on my arm. "But…not really." I fell silent, and thankfully he abandoned the subject.

We turned the corner and continued the art tour into the library. A bookshelf covered the whole west wall, up to the ceiling of the second floor, and a wooden ladder on gliding tracks reached all the way to the top shelf.

"I wonder how many kids they've had to coax down from that ladder," I said. My eyes followed the ladder up to the very top bookshelf, noticing several handwritten journals by KL Jones.

"Probably a few!" he said through a slight smile.

Then my attention was drawn to a framed five-by-seven black-and-white photograph of a small Hobie Wave sailboat, sailing away from the beach. Gently I picked it up.

Mrs. Jones walked toward us and said, "That was one of Mr. Jones's images that I found on the roll of film in his camera after he passed. I always loved his photography, and he loved using his film camera better than the digital. So I decided to have the film developed and framed some of his work to put around the house, but that is one of my favorites."

"When did you develop this film?" I asked, feeling almost queasy.

Mrs. Jones gave me a sideways glance before responding, "Maybe six months ago. He would set the boats up for our guests, and this allowed him to get to know the guests much better than I did. That may explain why I don't remember the two guests sailing in the picture, but my memory is not what it used to be." She sighed.

I brought the photograph closer to my eyes, taking in the two slight silhouettes that were sitting side by side. The taller girl's long blonde hair fluttered behind her as if she were in a movie. My hands went numb, and everything went dark.

"Rose. Rose, are you okay?" Mrs. Jones was asking me while Jes had his fingers on my pulse and looked at his watch.

When he looked back into my eyes, a flash of blue scrubs came into focus and disappeared as fast.

"Jess?" I said as the fog settled around me.

"Yes!" Jes replied.

"No! Jessica!" I turned my gaze to Mrs. Jones and immediately recalled her sitting at the piano playing. I blurted out, " 'And We Will Shine' by Dirk Maassen." I tried to stand but failed as I noticed Mrs. Jones's eyebrows rise like a question mark.

Jes placed his hand on my arm and said, "Hold up, you're not ready to stand up quite yet."

I stared into his eyes and knew I had seen him before. When I could, I slowly stood up and continued telling Mrs. Jones what was on my mind. "Kathie, I am so sorry I didn't tell you this before, but Jessica and I had an accident the day we were coming here, one year ago this week, the day after your husband died." I couldn't stop the tears, but my words continued. "Jessica and I were in the hospital for several days, but she didn't make it. I was in a coma." I felt Jes move away slightly, but I continued, "The photograph…she…me…sailboat." My last few words struggled out because I couldn't catch my breath. Tears uncontrollably flowed like rivers down my cheeks.

I think I have gone completely crazy!

Mrs. Jones picked up the broken frame from the floor and carefully looked at the image closer. "How?"

Jes saw Mrs. Jones's knees buckle and caught her arm. He guided her down into the reading chair, then gently took the photograph from Mrs. Jones and studied it.

She looked up at Jes and softly asked him to bring her journal over from the piano. The book's cover read: KL Jones. I have kept journals most of my life, I guess because if I didn't get my feelings out and on paper, sometimes I got overloaded with emotions and needed to retreat. It was also my way of empowering each day and gave me encouragement. And I realized I wasn't the only one. She flipped her journal open to the page she was looking for and read a journal entry out loud to us.

FRIDAY, 2ND OF APRIL

My love was here today—I felt him near. He's with a friend or two, and I heard, maybe felt them giggle. Their laughter told me that he's okay and gave me the strength to play our favorite song, the one we played together during all those years we shared. "Someone You Loved" by Lewis Capaldi.

Another stormy dark day, but at least today I saw a glimmer of your light.

Happy Anniversary, Charles. I miss you, my love.–Kathie

Jes's mouth hinged open slightly and then he asked me, "Rose, how did you get in this photograph when you have never been here before?"

I could only respond with a shrug. My head spun, my mind swirling with memories that I'd thought were dreams. "The week I was in the hospital"—I looked up at him knowing he would think nothing more than how crazy I sounded—"this photograph was taken that week. Jessica and Mr. Jones were trying to wait for me or trying to tell me something. I don't know." I tried hard to believe my own words as well when I said them aloud, but shook my head in disbelief.

"That's how you knew where my husband's secret ingredient was to add to the pasta sauce and how you learned to cut a pineapple the way he used to?" Mrs. Jones spoke softly.

I could only nod my head in response. *I guess I have been here before.*

Jes continued to stare at the black-and-white image, his mouth frozen slightly open. He swallowed hard and said, "I was called back to work because of an emergency the day after Mr. Jones passed. I hated to leave Kathie here alone after his passing, but I'm a doctor and I was on call." He softly touched Mrs. Jones's arm. "I worked in a hospital located only a few hours from here, and I remember it like it was yesterday. There were several people involved, but I was mainly working with the two college-age girls who were pulled from a terrible texting-while-driving accident. The driver texting was traveling north, crossed the median, flipped the car over into the southbound lanes." Jes paused for a second. "It was you. You were in a coma for weeks with a badly mangled arm and blunt trauma to the head. I heard the girl's car was unrecognizable. No one could believe the passenger—you—made it. The driver,

Jessica, fought hard for a few days, but…she was in terrible shape." His gaze locked on mine. "The ICU was slammed that week, so I was doing more than making rounds. Every nurse in the ICU called you a miracle. When you woke, you insisted you had been on spring break and had a hard time with reality for a bit. You were yelling for someone and then upset with your mother, and when I stepped into the room, you were trying to stand, but you turned white. I knew the look, so I rushed over to your bedside. That moment, you collapsed into my chest." He slowly brought his face down closer to mine and added, "It was me, Rose. Do you remember?"

My chest heaved in fear the air wouldn't fill my lungs ever again while my mind raced wildly. *The doctor in sky-blue scrubs.* "I remember the feeling more than the person I hugged," I said, but I remembered how the mystery man—Jes—had made me feel, the goosebumps that ran up and down my arms, the tingle, the sensation, the body shiver. My gaze never left his as the memories rushed through me. "The doctor in the hospital—you—when we touched, hugged, I felt at home and never wanted to let go, and yet, it didn't make sense. Nothing made sense. I was told my best friend Jessica was gone forever, and yet there I was, safe in your arms."

Carefully he placed the photograph of Jessica and me back on the shelf.

I watched him through the tears flowing from my eyes.

He turned to me, wrapped his strong arms around me, and whispered, "The fear and heartache may never go away, but I am with you. You will not have to go through this alone. I was with you then, as I am now."

We both turned to Mrs. Jones, who was smiling.

We stepped back and turned to listen to Kathie as she said, "Charles sent angels to be here with me, then and now."

I lifted my hand, holding an invisible glass up to Jessica and Mr. Jones. "Cheers to all the dreamers, the everyday believers. Here's to more of the everyday. Cheers!"

Dear Journal,

As I study more about empowering myself as an empath, I realize I want to enjoy my extraordinary gifts of sensitivity. My intuition and my intimate connection with spirituality brought me to the lake house where Jessica and I were to have an incredible spring break a year ago. The past year has been harder than hard. I had to force myself to finish the semester. Who am I kidding? For the longest time, I had to force myself to get up every morning.

On the hardest days, I could feel and hear Jessica saying, "Everything is going to be okay. I love you, Rose!" Whenever I heard this in my head, I replied out loud, "Ditto, Jess."

That brings me to today, because I am supposed to maintain an effective self-care practice, so I started journaling again. As I write, so many memories and feelings I once had are flooding over me. Today especially! Every inch of me misses her, and I have the full-fledged longing to run to Jessica and tell her everything that has happened today. But most of all, I want to run and find her on the float in the pool, jump on it with her, and say, "Guess what, Jessica? I met a boy! He has the most incredible deep-brown eyes…"

Funny thing is, just now when I wrote it down, I knew she heard me and smiled.

LAKEHOUSE DÉJÀ VU

Feeling: Blessed to have an angel as my best friend. A gifted Rose!

Dear Reader,

I hope you enjoyed reading *Lakehouse Déjà Vu*.

After I first laid eyes on the house my husband and I would soon make our new home, this story was envisioned over the course of multiple dreams. Although the house isn't a B&B, it became a place for Jessica and Rose to take a step into their future. It made me laugh and cry, but most of all, I came to realize how precious life is and how much we learn from everything around us—it's how we evolve and grow as humans.

Is there something or someone in your life—or a place—you realize is a gift that helped lift you up to blaze your own unique trail?

I would love to hear your thoughts about *Lakehouse Déjà Vu*.

Please return to your favorite online retailer to write a review.

ABOUT THE AUTHOR

RA Anderson is a wanderer who has lived all over, from California to Belize, and currently, her hew home is a town called Clermont! She grew up on horseback and sailboats—"the most amazing way to grow up!"

A lifelong passion for creative writing and photography became her life. Her award-winning photographs have been featured in table books, magazines, and front-page news, and her writing has been published in magazines, poetry books, Young Adult books and children's books.

Three boys—her heart and soul—call her Mom. She and her husband are recent empty-nesters, leaving them more time to travel.

"My life is full, colorful, and exhausting, and I wouldn't trade it for anything. However, people seem to think my most impressive accomplishment is that I know how to work the manual settings on a DSLR camera!"

https://ra-anderson.com/
https://www.facebook.com/raAndersonAuthor
https://www.instagram.com/ra_anderson_author/
https://twitter.com/Aruthanne

BOOKS BY
RA ANDERSON

CHILDREN'S

Once Upon the Rhine
(Cody the Cockatrice Series Book One)

The Land of Vikings & Trolls
(Cody the Cockatrice Series Book Two)

Puffins Take Flight
(Iceland: The Puffin Explorers Book 1)

Puffins Off the Beaten Path
(Iceland: The Puffin Explorers Book 2)

Puffins Encounter Fire & Ice
(Iceland: The Puffin Explorers Series Book 3)

Iceland: The Puffin Explorers Book of Fun Facts

ICELAND: The Puffin Explor-
ers Series Complete Set

YOUNG ADULT

Lakehouse Déjà Vu

The Last Crabtree Girl

Girl Sailing Aboard the Western Star

ALL READERS/COFFEE TABLE

If Pets Could Talk: A Service Dog

If Pets Could Talk: Farm Animals

If Pets Could Talk: Cats

If Pets Could Talk: Dogs